Compromised

Compromised

EMMY CURTIS

FOREVER
YOURS

New York Boston

Forever Yours
Hachette Book Group
1290 Avenue of the Americas
New York, NY 10104

forever-romance.com
twitter.com/foreverromance

First published as an ebook and as a print on demand: January 2016

Forever Yours is an imprint of Grand Central Publishing.

The Forever Yours name and logo are trademarks of Hachette Book Group, Inc.

The publisher is not responsible for websites (or their content) that are not owned by the publisher.

The Hachette Speakers Bureau provides a wide range of authors for speaking events. To find out more, go to www.hachettespeakersbureau.com or call (866) 376-6591.

ISBN 978-1-4555-6412-5

For the Chief, as always, with love and such.

Acknowledgments

I wanted to say a brief thank-you to the ladies in the Any Book Club, who have shown me a *really* good time in the few months I've been a member. Finding truly like-minded book people on a military base, in a foreign country, is a pure joy. Also, no one pokes fun at me for missing a deadline quite like these ladies. So thank you, everyone, with special appreciation for Leann Miller, Jamie Dakins, and Jaimee Strabala, who have already been coconspirators on a number of adventures: There were road trips, bookfairs, train fights, blood, and book signings. May there be many more!

Compromised

CHAPTER ONE

One year ago.

You got laid last night, didn't you?" Simon Tennant asked as he recognized the look on his friend's face. He'd seen it many times before. A cross between "holy hell, I'm lucky" and "what the fuck did I just do?" "I don't know how you do it, man."

Matt Stanning grinned as he fastened his seat belt. "Gotta love weddings," he said. "They make chicks crazy."

"But mine? You couldn't keep it in your pants until I was safely on my honeymoon? You better not have hit and quit one of Sadie's friends, or I'll never hear the end of it!" He was lying. His fiancée had a soft spot for Matt. In truth, Sadie had a soft spot for a lot of people; it was one of the things he loved about her.

Simon took a deep breath, barely believing *still* that she was about to become his wife. A sense of peace was blooming in his body, almost as if he were dying and being drawn to the light. No wait—way wrong analogy. He came up empty for anything better. He checked his watch. In four hours, Sadie Walker would become Mrs. Simon Tennant, and his life would finally be complete.

She was his anchor in the crazy world he worked in. The calm in the storm that raged through his professional life. After every mission, his only focus was getting home to her. Home. Sadie. He needed her in his life like a fire needs oxygen. He'd always thought that having a significant other would dull his desire to take the fight to the enemy, but that never happened. If anything, knowing he had her to come home to made him a better operative. Simply, his life was exponentially better with her in it. And he was about to make that permanent.

"So who was it?" He flashed a look at Matt, whose smile faltered just a little.

"You know, I'm not even sure she gave me her right name. Harry? Henrietta? Something like that." Matt was frowning now.

"She's Sadie's maid of honor. Her friends call her Harry," Simon said as he shifted down to turn on the road to Sadie's parents' house. He was a little intimidated to be in the home of the director of the CIA. As if getting married wasn't nerve-racking enough.

"Funny, she told me I should call her Henrietta."

Matt looked so perturbed Simon couldn't help but laugh. He was about to explain a little about her history, when he noticed the security barriers in the middle of Sadie's driveway were up, rendering it impassable.

"What's going on?" Matt asked as Simon pulled on the hand brake and got out of his car.

"No idea." Behind him he could hear Matt getting out of the car too.

"Excuse me," he called to a patrolling security man in black.

The man did a double take and looked around him as if seeking assistance. Then he placed his hand on his sidearm and approached the gate.

"Something's not right," Simon said in a low voice to Matt. Matt stayed silent.

"Can I help you?" the security man said in a careful voice.

"Hi there. Can we come in?"

"No one is allowed. Private. Come back later." The security man was sweating.

Simon could sense that Matt was about to explain that Simon was the groom, so he cut in. "Okay, no problem. We'll come back this afternoon."

They got back into the car and Simon threw it into reverse and slowly backed down the driveway. He rolled down his window and put the radio on loudly. As soon as he did that, the security man turned and walked away. There was nothing like music to divert attention and suspicion.

"Ukrainian?" Matt asked.

"I'd say southern Russian. He's not a member of the director's security team or the family's. Something's wrong."

Simon's Delta Force training immediately took over. He turned to Matt. "I'm going in."

Matt didn't hesitate. He shrugged out of his jacket and rolled up his sleeves. "How do you want to play this?"

"Not quite sure yet, but at least I've brought some toys to the party." Simon flashed a wolfish grin.

"Music to my ears."

Simon parked the car far enough up the road that it was out

of sight from the house. They jumped out as Simon popped the trunk with his fob and pulled aside the floor to reveal an array of small weapons.

"Dude, you shouldn't have," Matt said as if he'd been presented with the best gift ever.

Simon wanted to laugh, but in truth, he had only one thing on his mind and he was deadly serious about it: Get to Sadie. "Take extra ammo and the silencers. We have no idea how many of them there are."

They took their weapons of choice. "Are you absolutely sure we're not going to scale the wall and jump down in the middle of your mother-in-law-to-be's garden party?" Matt said.

It was possible. But his gut told him different. "You haven't met Sadie's mom. This would also be an entirely appropriate reaction to her." He chambered a round and held Matt's eyes. "You sure you're okay with this?"

Matt looked away, unconcerned. "Hey, this is what we do. Let's go get our girls."

Simon nodded once and the two approached the wall around the property, smoothly scaled it, and started scoping out the grounds as they made their way to the house. Sadie was in there.

His Sadie. If anything happened to her...

Simon slid around the side of the wedding tent in the backyard. As he rounded the front, he found two men, guns holstered and smoking. He showed himself, just on the slim chance that they were the director's guards. They went for their guns immediately, and he shot both of them in the forehead, barely registering the hits. He swung around instinctively to cover his back, but no one was there. He dragged the two men into the tent and closed the front flaps.

"Delta Lima, check in," a voice said over the walkie-talkie fastened to one of the men's belts. Answer or not answer?

Simon took a breath. "Da."

There was a long pause, and then the person at the other end clicked his SPEAK button in acknowledgment.

The tent flap moved, and he nearly took a shot. It was Matt. He needed to get a fucking grip on his emotions is what he needed to do right now.

"There are two on the right side of the house. One has a tablet or something that he seems to be monitoring. He's our mark, the one we need to question," Matt said, casting his eyes over the dead men on the ground.

"Copy that. It'll be my pleasure," Simon replied. The faster they got this done, the faster he could get to her. *Damn it—why didn't we elope?*

He exited the tent first. The lawn area was still empty. He ran for the house, so they could take the two men without the exposure of a direct approach. The guards were so focused on their tablet that Simon felt they could have just ambled up and asked them the time. Still, where was the fun in that?

He rounded the corner. "Hi there," he said.

About eight minutes later, they were inside the house, Simon taking the final kill-shot to end the immediate danger. "Where's Sadie?" he asked her brother, James. James pointed to the corridor behind him and Simon didn't hesitate. He needed eyes on her. As he approached her bedroom, she emerged, fear etched on her face.

"Oh my God, Simon. Thank God. I didn't know..." She dissolved into sobs that she stifled against his neck. His arms went around her. He was never letting her go. Never letting her out of his sight.

"Simon, we need you," James said. "My father is still in his study with two of the gunmen."

He looked up; Matt, James, and James's fiancée were all locked and loaded, waiting at the top of the stairs for him. "I have to go."

"No—don't leave me. Please don't leave—" she begged, and his heart just about cracked open. But Simon had no choice. It was his duty.

"I'll be right back. I promise."

She pulled away from him, makeup running down her face. "I can't, Simon. This..." she gestured at the dead man. "I can't..."

"Look at me. I'll be right back." He kissed her on the forehead and stalked down the corridor toward the others. He looked back as they took the stairs. She was hugging her younger sister, eyes squeezed shut, sobbing. A part of his heart fell away into darkness. Who would leave anyone suffering like that, let alone the woman he loved? But he had a duty. A duty to protect the United States from enemies, foreign and domestic. And country came first. Always.

Didn't it?

Ten minutes later, all the bad guys had been disposed of, but Sadie's brother had been shot. Simon ran from the scene to Sadie, but she was already outside staring at the dead bodies in the exact place they would have said their vows. One look in her eyes told him that they weren't going to get married that day.

"Sadie, please—just listen," he said, preempting anything that was going to come out of her mouth.

"I can't. I'm sorry. I see now what you do every day that you're not with me. This is what you do every time you leave me." She pointed at the knocked-over flower arrangements and the bloodstained aisle carpet.

"Please, I just need to explain—" An ambulance's sirens interrupted his plea.

Sadie's eyes flashed with horror. "Who...?" She looked at the front door.

Simon cursed himself. "I'm sorry; James was shot. I think he'll be fine, though."

"What?" She took a deep breath and then swallowed. "I have to go see him."

"I know." He could feel the distance between them already. He'd been worried about this the whole time they'd been dating. He never told her exactly what he did on a day-to-day basis. And now he'd never have to. It was here, in her family home, the dead bodies and blood that she would never be able to unsee.

"We'll talk. Later maybe," she said softly.

He reached in to kiss her good-bye, but she flinched away, shattering his heart into a million dark pieces. Suddenly he was alone, ice cold, with blood on his hands. Literally.

In that second, he knew with absolute certainty. No matter how much they'd talk, it would end the same way.

* * *

Sadie watched the nurses and doctors flit about the ICU with a detachment that she fought against. She needed to be here for her brother. Mentally and emotionally here.

She knew that no matter what she and Simon said, whatever they would discuss, it was over. The blood, his ability to leave her when she begged him not to, the *blood*. She'd known that he was in the black ops field of the army since the day she'd received her beautiful engagement ring, but now she'd seen him kill someone. Without giving his victim a second look. And then she'd gone outside and seen the blood all over the floorboards, carpet, and chairs where they'd expected to take their vows—she looked at her watch—two hours ago. There couldn't really be a clearer sign that this was not meant to be.

"Hey." His voice made her jump.

She looked up at him for a long time, not knowing what to say, where to start. Just seeing him there bought tears to her eyes. She had loved him so much. Maybe she still did, but his job was so dangerous, and so brutal, how long would it be before he was killed or something would happen that would change things for them forever? And even if it didn't, he would always be leaving her. He already treated his job as his wife and Sadie as his mistress, and now she knew for sure what he'd always left her for: death and destruction.

"Is he okay?" Simon asked as he sat next to her.

She nodded, looking straight ahead at the nurses' station, not daring to meet his eyes in case she just threw herself into his arms.

"But we're not, are we?" he said.

Sadie couldn't bring herself to nod or shake her head. Any movement would take the conversation somewhere she didn't want it to go, couldn't bear it to go.

"What happened? Look at me, damn it," he said, pain in his voice. "You can't just cut and run on our wedding day."

She took a deep breath, praying her voice wouldn't break and her chin wouldn't quiver, and turned toward him. "You cut and run all the time. When I had the flu, when we were just about to leave to go to Samantha and Jake's wedding, when we were supposed to take that vacation to Santa Barbara...movie dates, dinner dates. Your cell phone would chime and I knew I'd be on my own again. And I didn't mind too much. I knew you had an important job. But..." She swallowed, trying to keep her shit together. "Now I know what you do. Every time you leave me, it was to go kill someone, walk into danger...and I can't compete with that—I don't even want to."

Simon was silent, his eyes searching hers.

She blinked slowly and turned back around to face the nurses' station again. The nurse who had rushed James into the operating room appeared but didn't look at Sadie. When the nurse disappeared again, she turned back to Simon.

He was gone.

For a second she couldn't breathe, and then oxygen stuttered through her lungs and heaved out once, as sobs came from her stomach, her soul. He never once hesitated to fight for his country, but he refused to fight for her. She shook, and wept, and couldn't stop.

Not for a long, long time.

CHAPTER TWO

Present day.

Simon Tennant did a mental double take when he saw Sadie. He wasn't unprofessional enough to actually physically look at her again, but he ducked into a neighboring tourist shop to buy a postcard so he could take a breath and walk out and reassure himself that his brain must have been playing tricks.

Because there was absolutely no fucking way he'd just walked past his ex-fiancée, in fucking Athens, making out with another man. One who looked to be half Simon's age. Okay, maybe not half his age, but quite a few years younger. His fists clenched at the thought.

He walked past them again, reading the blank back of the postcard he'd just bought. Sure, her hair was shorter and lighter, but yeah, that was Sadie. Was she on vacation? What the hell was she doing there?

His brain struggled to get itself around the clusterfuck this whole trip had become. His assignment was supposed to be watching the Russian finance minister—keeping notes on whom the man met with and where he went. But most of Simon's intel so far was all about the guy's love life. He was having multiple freaking affairs and was trying to move around the city for his little rendezvous without being spotted.

And now, complicating things even more, Sadie was here too?

Well, okay then. She'd obviously moved on, and why shouldn't she have? He'd been a shit fiancé. Every time he'd needed her, she'd been there for him, and the times she'd needed him, his country had needed him more. Maybe he should have fought for her—he'd spent the best part of the past year wondering if he'd let go too easily—but he'd still have been in the same position: needing to defend his country. Calling off the wedding on the actual day had been a mutual agreement.

Okay, actually it had been her decision.

Then why haven't you moved on? He was concentrating on his work—that's what he'd been doing for the past year or so. He'd been promoted once and had been taking on more and more missions for CAG—what people usually thought of as the US Army's Delta Force.

Normally the missions were in war zones. Maybe 80 percent of the time. But sometimes something needed to happen on foreign soil that had to be able to be disavowed if the shit hit the fan. This was one of those occasions.

While Simon was keeping tabs on the Russian finance minister and getting the lay of the land, the rest of his team was gearing up. A four-man unit, they were virtually invincible. With the shorthand they'd developed, they barely needed to speak at all when the mission was hot. They'd worked with each other for so long that no one had to guess how the others would react to anything. It was the most comfortable he'd ever been.

Except for when he'd been in Sadie's bed. And heart. And...Fuck this shit. Nope. He wasn't concerned at all what she was doing here or whom she was doing it with. She was out of his head. Out of his everything.

Yeah, right.

* * *

When he stopped kissing her, Platon touched the front of her T-shirt with a smile. He loved her in it, which was why she'd been wearing that particular T-shirt—the one her father had banned her from wearing when she was sixteen—when she'd picked him up. Frankly, she was just happy it still fit, albeit a little tighter than it had been on her adolescent body.

"What are you doing tonight?" she asked him after taking her first sip of cold beer.

His eyes slid away from her. "Just meeting my friends. I should be free later if you want to get together."

Hmm. She smiled. "It depends how late it is...I have no idea what you do with your friends that takes so long." She pouted gently. She knew exactly where he would be. He'd be attending a meeting at a house in the Exarcheia neighborhood. The area was widely known as a hotbed for Greek anarchists. And it was her job to keep him close.

But Platon wasn't a regular anarchist—at least his group wasn't. As soon as the details of the G20 meetings had been released, along with the hotel where the dignitaries would be staying, Platon had applied for a job. The United States had picked up copies of all the new applications and profiled them. She had been part of the profiling team, working from her desk at the fake construction company she told everyone she worked at, but something had stuck out about this young man. Something had been off. The subjects he studied at school, the fairly high-paying jobs he'd had before he applied to be a security guard. It had tingled her "Spidey-sense," which is why she had made herself interesting to him.

She'd dug out her Hello Kitty T-shirt when Platon had spent half an hour in a Japanese manga store. She'd dyed her hair lighter when she'd seen him gravitate toward blondes. And donned glasses when she saw him do a double take at a girl in the street who wore a similar style. In short, she'd made herself perfect for him. Men were so easy.

"Tonight...might be difficult. I think it might be late by the time I finish. Too late for you, my hardworking girl." He smiled. "Unless you want to stay up all night and play hooky tomorrow. Is that what you call it? Hooky?" He pulled her closer to him and nuzzled her cheek.

God, she hoped he was right and wasn't confusing "hooky" with "hooker." "I wish I could, but you know my boss would fire me." She took a chance. "Stupid American."

She hadn't specifically told him she wasn't American, but

she had a Canadian flag on her backpack. "He's American?" Platon perked up a little, interest percolating in his eyes. "That explains why he works you so hard. Americans, they rely on slave labor, right? All over the world."

Ah. A typical anarchist talking point. She didn't answer him but leaned in to kiss him on his mouth. He groaned lightly and held her head to him as he slowly rubbed his semi-open mouth over hers. Teasing her, she supposed. She smiled against his mouth and let him kiss her again.

All Sadie's attention was on Platon. "Why don't we get together after your meeting?" She nuzzled his neck, feeling his pulse quicken beneath his skin. "Or maybe you can take me there? I want to share things with you, Platon. Don't you want to share things with me too?" The tip of her tongue flicked his earlobe.

His voice cracked under the suggestion. "Maybe. Maybe next time? I'll ask."

"You can tell them all about me...I don't mind," she said. She really wanted him to tell his friends that she was in the construction industry. No industry except arms dealing had more access to explosives than the construction industry. She thought that might make them interested in her.

"Maybe you can meet me outside this time?" His hand strayed to her thigh as he shouted something to their waiter.

The aproned man arrived with a piece of paper and a small pencil. Platon dashed down an address, different from the one she'd followed him to before. "Meet me here at ten tonight. I'll take you dancing after." His voice got husky, and she wondered if he was planning regular dancing or horizontal dancing.

She looked at her watch. "Okay, sweetie. I'll see you in a few hours. For dancing." She grabbed her bag, planted a kiss on the top of his head, and giggled a little as she squeezed out of their table. Her butt brushed against his arm as she slipped by him and she felt him lean into it.

As she walked away, turning and waving like a good girlfriend would do, she wondered how long and how far she could lead him on. She had to wait until she'd been at a meeting before she could turn him into an asset. He had to have something to lose. And that would be vouching for an undercover CIA officer at a meeting—her. From what she understood, the anarchist group he was into was less like a true political group and more like a motorbike gang—lawless and for hire. She was sure Platon had been placed inside the G20 hotel to wreak some damage to the meetings and the dignitaries attending them.

She needed to see her station chief.

CHAPTER THREE

Look, sweetheart, every CIA field officer rookie thinks they have a lead on some terrorist. Every single one. You're all fresh off The Farm, eager to make a difference, but ninety-nine percent of the time, you're just plain reaching." Director Lassiter bit down on the end of an unlit cigar, then made a face and pulled some tobacco from his mouth and grunted. "If these are Cubans, I'm fucking Fidel Castro."

Sadie Walker took a breath and wished she wasn't still wearing her Hello Kitty T-shirt. Nothing like a tiny pink T to confer gravitas and trustworthiness. "Sir, I'm not reaching. I've been talking to a man who is part of the security team at the hotel where the president will be staying, and—"

"Ms. Walker. You're here as a favor to your father. Don't make me regret that. By the way, is he coming over to visit? I have a few things I want to show him." For the first time that day he looked positively alert and eager.

Damn him. Damn her father, and damn the CIA. "Of

course, sir. I'll be sure to ask." Sadie quietly turned on the plush carpet and exited her boss's office. There was no point even trying to get through to him. And half of her wondered if her father, the director of the CIA, had asked her boss to keep her in an office somewhere out of the way. She wouldn't put it past him. He seemed supportive of her career change, but who really ever knew what he was thinking? He didn't become the director of the CIA by being easy to read.

Well too bad, Daddy. She'd just have to figure it out herself. Amass enough information that someone would listen to her, even if it wasn't Director Lassiter.

Until the previous October, she'd been an analyst at Langley, spending her days poring over documents, intercepts, and emails—trying to make links that would give field operatives around the world vital leads. But after her wedding had been rudely aborted by a gunfight at her father's house, she'd wanted to make a big change. Bigger than a new haircut, which she opted for when she realized she and Simon were over.

With an uncharacteristic disregard for her father's feelings, she'd applied for and been accepted into the training program at Camp Peary, the place CIA recruits call The Farm. She wanted to understand Simon, even though they'd broken up. Wanted to understand the clandestine, black-ops side of him that she'd only seen on the day of their wedding. Wanted to see how he could love his job but still want to marry her. It had been a mystery to her. An annoying, heartbreaking mystery. CIA clandestine ops were not usually dangerous, but the job would give her a front-row seat at how the black-ops side really worked. And maybe she would end up as strong as her brother's now wife, Beth, who had protected them all during the wedding-day assault.

Her first assignment posttraining was Athens, what some of her fellow recruits called a "soft" assignment. Which it was, no doubt. But this was the year that Greece was hosting the G20 meetings, which meant a constant yearlong rotation of politicians, bankers, scientists, economists, all with their differing agendas, and all with their differing protesters and threats. Bombs had already gone off, people killed, and the Russians were up to something involving a "new vision for Europe"— scary in itself, she thought. A tension had pervaded the city, taking no prisoners and leaving everyone on edge.

On edge, and reeling from the extreme heat wave that was washing through the city like a tsunami. Except, it seemed, her damned boss, who didn't seem to care about anything other than his golf swing. But following last week's series of bombs, an attempted murder of an American citizen, and not to mention the accidental assassination of a Russian minister by his own intelligence agency, Sadie's gut told her something was going on in her city, and her blood pressure rose every time she caught Director Lassiter reading *Golf Digest* on a conference call or taking the afternoon off to "slip in a quick nine" with his golf buddies. It was like he was running a scout troop instead of an intelligence-gathering organization, and it made her madder than hell.

When she'd been given an encrypted thumb drive by an asset the previous week, she'd given it to him, and he'd just thrown it into an in-tray on his filing cabinet, exactly where Sadie had found it five days later, with coffee requisition invoices and a reservation printout for a golfing holiday on top of it. She'd taken the drive back and he hadn't even noticed.

Anger started rising in her chest again as she thought about it. If the stupid man paid half as much attention to his work as he did to golf, acquiring cigars, and asking when her father was coming to visit, he might be a useful person to have around.

She went back to her desk and started packing up for the day, wondering if the director was right about her and Platon. Maybe she was just being a rookie. Her job in Athens was to develop contacts in all parts of society. She'd made one. Platon. She'd forced a meet with him at a touristy bar in the Plaka area of the city, and they'd spent the evening flirting and talking about their jobs.

Sadie, of course, had told him only about her cover job—a low-ranking executive at a multinational construction company—and he had told her about his new job as a security guard at the G20 hotel. But she was fairly certain he was involved with a local group of anarchists who had firebombed some local American companies in the city. She intended on finding out exactly what was going on with him, hopefully way before the president of the United States had feet on the ground in Greece.

She'd followed Platon for two weeks, seeing where he went at night, whom he talked to, and on the fourteenth evening, she'd dressed exactly the same as the girls he was usually hitting on in the bars, and ensnared him. And that was how female field officers often had it easier than men.

In the two weeks since then, she'd been available, but not too available, and interesting, but not too interesting. She thought her refusal to sleep with him was keeping him eager enough for now. She'd been trained to do that at The Farm, but it was a fine line to walk.

A line she had no intention of crossing.

CHAPTER FOUR

He remained in the shadows as Sadie let herself into her tiny apartment. He wanted a second to watch her before making his presence known.

When Simon had let himself in, all the shutters had been closed, leaving the room much cooler than it had been outside in the afternoon sun. But as soon as he had eyes on her, he felt the temperature rising uncomfortably.

He was about to step out of the shadows, but barely before she'd put her purse down, she'd stripped off her crazy Hello Kitty T-shirt and unzipped her denim skirt. Even if he wanted to, he couldn't say anything. Her body looked stronger than it had the last time he'd seen her naked. Dammit. His dick twitched in reaction to the new Sadie. Her shorter hair, the way it framed her face. Her long legs and full breasts. He blinked, thinking about the days and nights they'd spent together. It felt like years ago. It felt like yesterday too. His fingers itched to touch her; his mouth watered to taste her again.

Sadie flopped on the bed, arms and legs splayed to take advantage of the ceiling fan's downdraft. She moaned as the air touched her skin. He watched as her nipples grew in the cool air. Goddamnit, this was obscene. He couldn't stand here getting off. Why didn't she stay in her freaking clothes? She stretched and...he couldn't take any more.

He cleared his throat, and she jumped up.

"What the...?"

He stepped forward with his hands showing. Force of habit. He doubted Sadie had the wherewithal to shoot him.

"Who is...Simon? *Simon?* What the hell? What are you doing here...in my apartment? What?" She looked around her as if looking for something to hit him with.

He grabbed her silky robe from the chair in the corner and handed it to her, the other hand still aloft. All her questions were valid, for sure. He didn't know why he'd been hoping for a slightly warmer welcome. Or even a welcome at all. He knew they'd parted on...if not bad, then awkward terms.

And he'd just witnessed her moving on with that young kid.

"How dare you..." She struggled into her robe and tied it so tight that he was surprised she could breathe. He made the mistake of smiling at the thought. "What the fuck do you think you're doing here? Did you"—she looked at the door—"did you break into my home? What the fuck is wrong with you?" Her eyes blazed with an intensity he'd never seen before. Especially not directed at him. "Get out. Get the *fuck* out." She crossed her arms as if to punctuate the sentence.

She was so sexy when she was pissed. "I saw you in the street but didn't want to interrupt you..." He let the sentence trail off just enough to let her know where he'd seen her. He didn't really know why it was important, but somehow it just was. Why the hell was he here? He started to get that itchy feeling as if he were about to be ambushed. It was an instinct that had served him well in the field. He sighed. "You're right. I just didn't want to blow my cover by talking to you in public. I shouldn't have let myself in. It's just...almost second nature to me now. I'm sorry. I'll go."

He waited a second for her to protest, but she didn't. Her eyes just narrowed infinitesimally. Even her facial expressions had changed. Before, her whole face was open to laughter, sadness, happiness—everything was written clearly on her face. But now he hesitated. He couldn't get a read on her at all. It was like she wasn't the Sadie he'd known. Was she in some kind of trouble? Was that why she was in Athens? But no. Remembering her snuggling up to that...that boy—nothing about that had seemed stressful to him. "Good-bye, Sadie. It was good to see you again."

In a second, before he'd even thought about it or considered some kind of game plan, he'd taken two strides toward her, snaked an arm around her waist, and pulled her to him. His mouth descended on hers, as she opened it to exclaim. Her hot breath and soft lips—the very smell and taste of her felt like home. Had always felt like home.

Even from the first time he'd engineered their meeting.

His kiss claimed her as his. *Always his.*

And then as quickly as he'd gained entry, he left.

CHAPTER FIVE

Sadie's blood chilled as the door closed. She perched on the edge of her bed and dug her fingers into the sheets. Why was he here? A gnawing in the pit of her stomach made her rub her belly and wince. Why had he come? How dare he kiss her like that—as if he still had the right. How had he gotten in? She thought she knew enough to secure her home, but obviously she didn't know as much about Simon and his skills as she'd thought.

That wasn't a surprise, though. Her first week of training at The Farm had told her all she needed to know about her relationship with the man she'd nearly married.

She'd been his mark.

She remembered the lesson well. How to establish trust. You wait for a moment where you could easily take advantage of someone, and you don't take advantage of them. Then you wait for them to call. She'd sat in that class, chilled to the bone, knowing that she'd almost married someone who had followed this training to a T.

Mumbai, 2012

Sadie was running over her PowerPoint one last time before she presented her analysis on terrorist movements to the Asia bureau chief. It was supposed to be a whistle-stop visit—just a one-night stay—but she'd jumped at the chance of going to India. It wasn't until she was on the plane, facing thirteen hours in coach class, that she realized she probably only had gotten the opportunity because no one else had wanted to go. Oh, the joys of being the lowest on the totem pole.

She'd had only enough time to dump her bags at the hotel, touch up her makeup, and run through the presentation one more time before walking the two blocks to the embassy. She stopped in front of the building to root around in her bag for her ID, when the ground shook under her feet. A blast sounded a split second after, and she watched in numb horror as the windows of the building opposite the embassy blew out onto the street. There was a second of silence, punctuated only by the soft sprinkle of glass on the concrete street. Then muffled screams. Hers.

Blood covered her hands, and pain radiated through her. She catalogued all the pain before she realized she was lying against the wall of the embassy. A man stooped over her, sliding his hands efficiently over her limbs before helping her up. She recognized him. He'd smiled at her several times on the flight from Los Angeles. She'd smiled back.

"You're okay. Can you stand up?" he said, gently nudging her upright. The pain seemed to fade as he smiled at her again.

"Thank you." Her own voice sounded thick to her ears as she

struggled to her feet. She took a second to steady her legs and then looked up—way up—to meet his eyes. Even with her heels on, he was tall. He'd looked muscly on the plane, but she'd assumed every man who stood up in a plane looked big. Now she knew different. He had a little scruff, probably from traveling, and hair that was a little longer than a neat haircut. His intense blue eyes radiated concern, but all she wanted to do was run her fingers through his sandy-colored hair and see if it was as thick as it looked.

"Do you want me to call for an ambulance? Or do you want to go back to your hotel? I think the embassy will be on lockdown for a while."

"Hotel," she croaked, before coughing. Dust seemed to coat the inside of her mouth.

"You probably need a drink too. Maybe a bunch of them." He carefully wrapped his arm around her, under her shoulder, and supported her back to her hotel. Her head was still full of bleeding people, screaming, and the echo of the loud boom played and replayed.

"I think I need to drink a lot," she said, feeling better that she'd made a firm decision.

"Excellent idea." He escorted her to the bar in the lobby and sat her down. The waitstaff looked at her worriedly as her rescuer ordered them some drinks. He came back to the table with a bottle of brandy and two glasses.

"Brandy?" she asked.

He looked a little concerned. "It seemed...medicinal? At least more medicinal than the mojitos they're famous for here." He looked again at the bottle. "I'm sure this is the right thing for shock. *Women in old movies were always prescribed a stiff brandy for shock, right?"*

Sadie laughed and then winced as her cut lip cracked with the effort. *"I guess. Hey, do I really look that awful? People are looking at me weirdly."* She fluttered her fingertips over her lip and the place on her brow that was sore.

He shook his head, and she enjoyed a second of relief before he continued. *"Honestly, you look like you've done five rounds with Tyson. But you still look beautiful. Just scary. Hard-core even. Dripping blood looks great on you."* He smiled and handed her a glass. He clinked his against it. *"Here's to survival, and a coincidental meeting."*

She clinked it back and took a sip. Fire slipped down her throat. It felt good. Really good. She held her glass out for another, and this time he half filled her glass—double the shot she'd finished in seconds.

"Do you think I need to go back and...I don't know, say I'm a witness?" she asked after she'd nearly finished her second glass.

"Did you see anything?" he asked, refilling his own brandy.

"No. I don't think I did," she admitted.

"Then I'd just wait for things to calm down and call the embassy in a few hours and tell them what happened." He held the bottle up and she nodded.

Warm liquid was pooling at her knees and her aches and pains started receding into the alcohol. He was so cute. So funny. They laughed and drank. Until she yawned.

"You should probably try to get some sleep. Jet lag combined with nearly exploding will do that for you."

She giggled and tried to stand up. He jumped up to steady her.

"I'll help you to your room. God only knows what you'll get your-self into if I leave you here."

Suddenly she thought, you. I want to get into you. She leaned up and kissed him. First a small experimental kiss. And then when he didn't pull away and his hands dropped to her waist, she kissed him properly. Euphoria pumped around her as his tongue slid against hers.

Rationally, she knew exactly what this was. It was a happy-to-be-alive euphoria driven by adrenaline and alcohol. She didn't care. He was sexy and funny and he'd rescued her. After all, she'd sort of known him from the plane. That totally counted, right? Even as she had the thoughts, she knew they were a pure excuse; she just didn't care.

She opened the door with her key card and he helped her in. She kissed him again, feeling the tipping point where she would be lost in him. His mouth, his scent, his warmth. She leaned in, but he squeezed her arms and took a step back.

"Should I call a doctor for you? You have a few cuts and bruises, but nothing that looks serious," he said, still not crossing the threshold.

"I'll be fine; thank you," she managed to say before shakes racked her whole body. Her teeth clattered together as if she'd been in an ice bath.

Concern flashed across his face. He walked her to the bed, with his arm under hers, supporting her. She allowed him to wrap bed-clothes around her and lay her down.

"What's your name?" she whispered, as sleep washed over her.

"Simon." His voice sounded as if it came from a million miles away.

She later woke up in the same clothes as she'd fallen asleep in. A glass of water and some ibuprofen were on the bedside table, along with a note on hotel stationery. Just his name and a number.

She thought him so honorable. So good not to have taken advantage of her. She had all but thrown herself at him.

* * *

Present day

It didn't occur to her to even question how he knew which hotel she'd been in until she'd been in her class at The Farm. She'd been so stupid.

Simon didn't make a sound as he left her apartment building.

She grabbed a baggy T-shirt as if that would stop the feeling of vulnerability. She'd kissed him back. *What the hell was that all about?* When they'd called off the wedding and he'd all but disappeared, she'd rehearsed a dozen different ways she would act if she saw him again. Frosty, flippant, blasé. Not one of them involved a kiss that rated on the cellular level. She touched her fingers to her lips and replayed it.

She should have been immune to his kiss; his presence should have been nothing more than an annoyance. She knew who he was now. Knew he'd used tradecraft to meet and date her. But all that knowledge hadn't stopped her from melting when he kissed her. Hadn't stopped her from not punching him. *Dammit.*

The only thing she held on to was that her training kicked in and she'd been able to dial back her instinct to grab her weapon from under her pillow. As a CIA field officer, she wasn't supposed to have any kind of firearm. The agency recruited her because she could use her head. She was supposed to be able to avoid any situation that might be dangerous and extricate herself from anything that became dangerous. Her brain was her weapon. That's what they drilled into her at The Farm. But her brother had visited and found a way to slip her a brand-new Glock.

Simon would have known something wasn't right if he'd seen her with a gun. The last thing she wanted to do was blow her cover. She knew he worked for CAG, but that was because last year they'd been engaged. The fact that he didn't know that she was a field officer now gave her a measure of satisfaction, not to mention a big advantage over him, whatever he was doing in Athens.

What *was* he doing there? Not a vacation, that was for sure. He must be in the city for something to do with the G20. But what the hell would Delta Force be doing on the ground? That unit didn't deploy unless they had a specific mission and a specific time frame to accomplish it in. They didn't just cruise a city until something happened.

She moved slowly through the cool room, touching the few ornaments and photos she had, not really thinking about them but how Simon might play into her situation with Platon. If at all. Did he see them together because he was watching Platon? A finger of excitement danced at the base of her spine. That would mean that she was right. But if they were onto the same potential plot, there was no way on God's earth she was going to let him snatch the lead away from her. Platon was *her* mark.

Speaking of which. She glanced at her bedside clock and ran for the shower. She had to think about what she should wear to meet Platon. The problem was the intense heat. In the winter she wore boots in which she could keep a multitude of sins: backup cell phone battery, retractable carbon baton—her weapon of choice—or even a European-style flick knife. If they let her into the meeting, they were certain to frisk her, or at least look in her bag. She batted ideas back and forth and decided on a sundress and a clutch purse big enough for her cell phone and some euros. Better to foster an image of being no threat than to give them anything to wonder about. In fact...she would add some condoms to her purse too. If they saw those, they would be sure that she was just Platon's girlfriend. She smiled to herself as she slipped on her sundress, and as a nod to practicality, she pulled on some matching bike shorts that just peeked out under the hem of the dress. A chastity belt by any other name.

Before she left, as she always did before going out "on the job," she opened her laptop and encrypted a short paragraph about where she was going, what she hoped to achieve, how long she thought she'd be gone, and the cell phone number of the burner phone she was using for this mission. She sent the file to the office central database and headed out.

CHAPTER SIX

Simon was in his hotel room speaking with his boss on his secure iPhone, trying to keep his mind off Sadie and on the matter at hand. It should have been easier than it was.

"I'm sorry, sir. You're breaking up," he faked.

"The director of the local office said one of his less-experienced associates had been passed intel—or a rumor, the director assures me—that there is some kind of plot to snatch the Russian finance minister from the conference. As far as I can tell, it's not us..." Even to Simon's ears, he sounded skeptical. "But the intel seems to only come from Russian assets, so read into that what you may."

What he read into it was that it could be a Russian plan to blame the US and galvanize their people to support a war in Ukraine, Chechnya, or even America. Nothing would incense the Russians more than the abduction of a member of the government, especially if they were told that the US was responsible. "Roger that."

"Just watch him, Tennant. That's all you're authorized to do at this point. Your team will be en route in a couple of days. Then we can talk about counterplanning. Just remember, we've got no allies in Athens right now."

He remembered all right. Until his team arrived, Simon was on his own. "Understood. I'm low-pro, just going by the numbers until the guys get here."

"Barnum out," his boss said, before his screen went black.

Yes, they joked that Barnum ran the circus, and sometimes his job felt like that, but they always got the mission tucked away.

He put his phone on the alarm clock / iPhone dock to charge. This was the nicest hotel room he'd been in on the job since Nigeria. His mouth twitched as he remembered his infamous escape, on a donkey, in a fetching purple dress and hijab. Let it never be said he didn't do what it took to get the job done.

He pulled back the drapes in the main room of his suite and looked out across Syntagma Square to the government buildings. He distracted himself from thoughts of Sadie by planning a hypothetical attack on the Greek government building. It was a habit that exercised the parts of his brain he hadn't used a whole lot since his CAG training. It was one that lulled him into his comfort zone.

He split the square into grids and mentally blew up a trash can halfway down the pattern. He imagined the police guarding the government building would come running, because they would feel like they could get to injured people easily. If he blew the trash can at the back of the square, they would probably wait for other responders.

When they left their posts, he would use stick-and-set explosives in the guard hut and throw some low-grade smoke bombs in through the courtyard.

Just as he pictured ancillary staff running out of the courtyard away from the smoke, his mind settled on one person running. Sadie. Her body had seemed different to him. Harder? More defined maybe. She'd always been a runner—and Jesus, did she look hot when she was running: sweaty, flushed, and out of breath—but this wasn't just a runner's body. Maybe she'd taken up Pilates since their breakup. Women did that kind of thing, he was sure.

Almost sure.

He turned away from the window, his concentration shot.

He headed for the shower and put the new Sadie—with her Pilates body and shorter, lighter hair—into an old scene. A long weekend vacation in Mexico. For him it had been work, but she'd had no idea the rest of his team had been there. And that he hadn't just sat on the beach while she was in the spa for three hours. But he remembered the feel of her when he returned. Soft and slightly oily, flushed with relaxation, and half-closed eyes. He'd slowly undone her terry spa robe and let it fall. She'd stood there fighting the impulse to cover herself as she usually did. Her skin was cool and damp under his fingertips. She'd bitten her lip when he'd stroked those nipples into hard tips. Moaned lightly when he gently bit them. And when he'd laid her back and penetrated her still with his pants on, fresh from the mission, she'd closed her eyes and rocked her pelvis just enough for him to reach for his climax. Her breasts bobbed with every thrust, mouth slightly open, totally responsive to his every move.

Now, he swallowed hard with the memory as he stroked himself in the shower, one arm supporting himself against the tiled wall as his body reacted to the image of her on her back, taking him inside her, as he stood between her soft thighs.

He bit back a groan as he came, heat threading through his legs, making them shake. Sighing, he finished washing himself, then pushed the control toward cold and stood beneath the cool water, trying to realign his thoughts to the mission at hand. He had one last check to do on the Russian finance minister before he could call it a night.

* * *

Sadie stood beneath a tree outside the address Platon had given her. She'd started out by standing under a lamppost, but after a couple of catcalls from kids, she'd realized her error. The street was like any other Athenian residential street, the house like all the others. For a brief second she doubted herself and wondered if this was just where his parents lived. But no. She'd done meticulous research into his family. No one in the Asker family lived here.

Her phone clock said that she was on time, even though she'd spent a little time avoiding what the teachers at The Farm called the "Angelina Jolie effect"—looking too perfect and therefore standing out. To negate that, the female officers were trained to choose two or three things that would subconsciously persuade people that they were of no threat. One of her colleagues always had toothpaste on the front of her shirt—at least now, come to think of it, she *guessed* that was her anti–Angelina Jolie method. Maybe she just always dribbled. Sadie smiled to herself. But it had worked. People took one look at her and dismissed her as a harried young mother.

Sadie had chosen abject clumsiness. That manifested itself with slightly smudged lipstick, and when she thought someone was looking, she'd stumble or walk into something or someone. The latter made her pretty adept at the shoulder swipe, where you brushed past someone with enough force to allow a colleague to take something from their jacket or bag. She'd always figured that if the CIA didn't work out for her, she'd do pretty well as a pickpocket.

She looked at the time again. A field officer would wait patiently. But a girlfriend wouldn't. She texted him:

You forgot about me???

A minute later his head popped around a door that he held closed against his body. Excitement trickled through her. What was he hiding inside? She waved and pointed at her bare wrist, to indicate the time. She pouted, which made him grin and beckon to her.

He didn't open the door for her but instead held up a finger. "We do very important work here, so don't talk to anyone unless they talk to you. These things we discuss are not for women—do you understand? I don't want you to get into any trouble." He looked so uncertain and unsure of what he was doing that she gave him a pass on the whole "men's work" thing.

She widened her eyes as if she were impressed. "Of course not. I'll be a mouse; I promise." She pursed her lips together, closed her eyes, and leaned in for a peck. "Can we go dancing after?" she asked, again designed to make him think that her concern was dancing and not the meeting he was attending here.

He grinned—a sweet smile she was beginning to like—and nodded. "Of course. I know just the place."

She made her eyes widen in glee. "Where? Where are we going?" she asked as she made a step inside, forcing him to open the door for her.

"I'll tell you later. We should be done here in about twenty minutes. Go sit over there." He pointed at a row of meeting room–style chairs, placed back against the wall. In fact, the whole small reception room of the house looked more like a meeting room than someone's residence. There were no decorations—just a table at the front and these chairs in rows. Almost like a schoolroom. The Spartan atmosphere made it even more likely that this was an organizational hub for the group of anarchists that Platon was somehow involved in. God, she hoped she was right and that he wasn't just taking evening classes in something.

She counted seven other men in addition to Platon. An eighth man came in from what she could see was a very old kitchen. He was sipping coffee from a tiny cup. Deep lines creased his face and thick white hair was cut short—almost marine short. He was definitely the boss. His steely gaze rested on her immediately. A chill seeped through her toes through her legs. He was not a good man; she instinctively understood this. And if nothing else, she'd been taught to rely on her gut. In practice sessions she had scored an 87 percent success rate when she made decisions based on her instinctive reaction to a training scenario. Most others hovered around 60 percent. She'd figured it was in her genes.

As much as she wanted to run away from his glance, she smiled instantly, wide-eyed and guileless. She really didn't want to be on the wrong side of him without a weapon. He nodded slightly and she went to work on a cuticle, feigning boredom.

While she picked at her nail, she mentally filed what she had already seen. The men were all big guys. If she didn't know any better, she would have thought they were New Jersey dockworkers or something similar. The docks. Of course. That would explain how the anarchists got their weapons and explosives.

Pride spiked through her as she tried to pick up what they were saying, but they were talking too fast for her to get a good sense of the conversation. She cursed her postponement of her immersive language course. It didn't help when practically 80 percent of Greeks spoke better English than she did Greek. She should have known better. Why would criminals plot in a foreign language? This wasn't an effing movie.

"What is the matter, young lady?" He-Man growled from the front of the room.

Her head popped up at the sudden English. And the rumble of his words.

"I'm...I'm sorry?" she replied, flashing a quick look at Platon. His grimace did not comfort her.

"You were frowning quite determinedly. What were you thinking?" He moved around the men, who were now craning their heads in their chairs, and grabbed one, sitting astride it less than a foot away from her.

She affected a tiny pout. "Platon promised to take me dancing, and I was wondering when you'd be finished."

The men laughed. But not the leader.

"Where are you from?" As he asked the question, he slowly turned his head back to Platon as if to make it clear that he was double-checking his answers.

Sadie had never so much wished for her baton. She had this nasty thought that if she said the wrong thing she would never be found again. "Manitoba?" she squeaked out.

Manitoba? Fuck. She didn't know anything about Manitoba. Rookie, rookie, *rookie* mistake.

"Canada." He nodded to himself as if he was formulating a plan. "Yet Platon tells me you work for an American company. Is that right?"

She frowned as if she had no idea what he was getting at. "Yes. For now I do." *Now we are back to solid ground.* "I'm...I'm just an inventory clerk, though."

She saw it in his eyes. A spark that told her she'd said exactly the right thing. And that told her that she'd been right in her suspicions of Platon. Her eyes flickered to him. So young in this group of older men. She wondered for an instant if he really understood what he was up to his neck into.

"You do important work," the old man crooned.

"No, not really. My boss is the only important one in the office. Just ask him!" she said, aiming for some kind of common ground, making it easy for him to think he was creating a rapport with her.

He laughed, and then the others laughed too. "I like her." He turned his head, acknowledging Platon again.

He stood, turning the chair the right way again. "You must tell us if your boss disrespects you. We will be proud to show him...the error of his ways." He held his hand out, palm up.

She placed her hand in his and he kissed her knuckles. "Thank you...?" *Tell me your name. Tell me your name.*

"You can call me Stratigos." He nodded and turned away.

Dammit. Stratigos was Greek for "general."

Platon seemed to hold eye contact with Stratigos as he walked by, nodding slightly as he did so. What message had they passed between them?

He beckoned her with his index finger and smiled, nodding toward the door. She wanted to stay, try to record some of what they were saying, but she knew she'd made enough progress there already. She needed to play it carefully. Get pushy or too involved and they would be suspicious. Far better to keep Platon happy and stay safe.

As soon as the door closed behind them, Sadie had to work hard to rein in her exuberance. Screw the director...she'd been right! This had been her first time actually working as a field agent, and it had been a success. She was so psyched that when Platon spun her around to kiss her, she kissed him back. Properly. Passionately. They kissed and she tried to feel something. Anything, really, that would tell her that there were other guys whose kiss could make her feel like Simon's did. She tried to channel the euphoria of the successful contact with Stratigos into the kiss.

Nada.

He picked her up and pressed against her, which brought

her crashing back to her senses. What the hell was she doing? He was a mark, nothing more. She wrenched herself away from his lips, painfully aware that she had crossed a line. She smiled at him, surreptitiously pressing the volume button on her phone, making it chirp.

"Sorry—I should get that," she said breathlessly, holding up her phone. "Hello?" she said to no one. "Of course, sir. Yes, sir. I'll be there...yes, I'll be there as soon as I can." She glanced ruefully at him and shrugged. "I've got to go. I'm so sorry. My boss..."

"It's all right. I understand tough bosses. I have to work an extra shift tonight too. One of our night porters is sick. I was hoping we would get a little dancing in before I had to go. But it is just as well. Do you want me to walk you to your office?" he asked, holding her hand in front of him, half giving her the impression that he was going to kiss it like Stratigos did.

"No, sweetie. It's still early; I'll be fine."

"Go with God, darling," he replied in that sweet, formal Greek way of his.

She looked back once or twice to find him watching as she left. She waved and he waved back. He was so young. She'd just totally kissed a twenty-two-year-old. She grinned. She'd been right about Platon, and she was actually getting positive results. Her boss could kiss her ass. All she needed now was to have them ask her for explosives and she'd have enough to make Lassiter listen to her.

She virtually skipped up her apartment steps, anxious to do something—write a report, scream, or dance. She had to do something...she felt like she'd explode.

CHAPTER SEVEN

Tennant? I didn't expect to hear from you, son."

"I'm sorry to disturb you, but it's about Sadie." She would never speak to him again if she found out he was speaking to her father.

"Is she all right? What's going on?" His voice was strident, a man who was used to being in charge and getting answers.

Shit. He hadn't thought this one through. He couldn't tell the director of the CIA that he'd been deployed to Athens. That would get his ass fired and his boss in front of Congress in record time. What was it about her that made him forget everything else? Dammit.

"I'm sorry, sir. Don't worry. Sorry again to have bothered you."

"Don't you dare hang up on me, Tennant. You tell me what is going on or I'll have you in the brig faster than you can say 'ex-fiancé.'"

Simon had no idea what she'd told her father about their

breakup, but since he'd paid for a very large wedding that didn't happen, he figured at the very least he was on the director's shit list. "I heard that Sadie was in Greece. She's been seen with someone of interest...I mean, someone we have a file on. I'm worried she might be in danger." There was no way he was explaining that he'd spent hours looking at candid shots of everyone "of interest" in Greece that nestled in CAG's classified computer files. Simon had found Sadie's boyfriend in a photo with an explosives expert. He knew it could be nothing. But it could also be something.

"Now you listen to me, young man. If I find out you're keeping tabs on my daughter, they will never find your body. Do you understand?"

"Yessir," he said and disconnected the call. There was nothing else he could say under the circumstances. He really should have played that whole thing out in his head before he picked up the damn phone. He gritted his teeth. Sadie...even when they were apart she could fuck him up.

All he could do was talk to her. Warn her away from this Platon Asker. Not that he had a firm grasp on why. I mean, he was sure he'd been pictured with some unsavory characters too. But this was Sadie. His Sadie, whether she accepted that or not. He wasn't going to sit around and let her get mixed up in anything dangerous. Even if it meant getting fired from his own job.

The finance minister was already back at his hotel room with his wife, and Simon prayed she would keep him there. Right now, he had to go see Sadie. Properly this time. He'd knock and everything.

In ten minutes he was at her door with a bottle of ouzo. He put his ear close to the door as he raised his hand to knock. Force of habit, he guessed. But he'd definitely heard something. Not a television or radio—what was that?

It was a moan. Was she hurt? Even before he'd finished the thought, let alone considered the fact that she might have someone with her, he put his shoulder to the door in exactly the weakest point and shoved. The door blew open and Sadie gasped, sitting up ramrod straight in bed.

"What the—? Simon? What the fuck?" She jumped off the bed and ran at him, as if she could push him out. He didn't move.

"It sounded like you were hurt. Look—I came with a peace offering." He held up the bottle.

"Get out! Get out! Did you follow me here? To Greece? How dare you! Get out!" She barely caught a breath before she tried to shove him toward the door. When he didn't move, she slapped his chest, and in that second he knew what she'd been doing. He could smell her unique scent on her hand, her fingers. He grabbed her hand to stop her from hitting him again, and inhaled.

"What were you doing?" he ground out, holding her hand in front of his face.

"Oh my God..." she half moaned, half shouted. A flush radiated from her neck up to her face. She tried to snatch her hand away, but he wouldn't let her. Instead, eyes on hers, he pulled her to him and put two of her fingers into his mouth. His eyes closed, lost in memory. Her taste hadn't changed—sweet and salty and musky. He felt his utter arousal start clouding his mind.

"Stop. Simon." She struggled against him. He released her hand immediately. What was the matter with her? There was a fire in her eyes he'd never seen before, an intensity, a confidence that she simply had never possessed last year. "What are you doing?"

"I came by to warn you about the boy you've been hanging out with," he said between gritted teeth.

Her eyes narrowed. "He's not a little boy."

Score. "I didn't say 'little.'" He couldn't help but smirk at her. He wasn't expecting her fist to come flying at his jaw. Not even a little. He pulled back, just enough to take the power out of the punch, but it still hurt. His feelings mostly. No one had landed a punch on him for a good number of years.

"Really? That's what I get for coming to warn you..." he began.

She poked her finger at his chest. "You don't get to warn me about anyone. You lost that right ages ago. You lost the right to come into my room, to bring"—she looked at the bottle he'd thrown onto the bed—"the cheapest brand of ouzo you could find..."

Well, that stung. He must have been ripped off by the shopkeeper. He was about to tell her how much it cost him, but there was something in her eyes. Something he kind of recognized but that was different. *She* was different. Sadie had never been combative. She'd been passive. A perfect CAG wife, as everyone had said. He'd never been too sure. And right now, she wanted something. From him. He was sure.

"So what are you going to do about it?" he asked.

"Teach you a lesson," she hissed.

"Oh ye—" he began.

She grabbed his T-shirt on his chest and fisted it, twisting and pulling until he was touching her. She kicked the door shut behind him and pushed him toward the bed.

"Okaaaaay," he drew out. Was it really that easy? He really didn't want to misread the situation. He had the idea there would be no coming back from this if he took to her bed, when really all she was about to do was call the cops.

"Don't talk to me," she said. "I don't want to hear your lying, cheating voice."

What?

* * *

Blood was rushing to parts of Sadie that she couldn't stop. Her face was burning, and so were other parts. She knew it was the postmission adrenaline high making her so horny. How convenient that Simon just happened to show up at the door. Fucking him would complicate things, for sure, but she really didn't care: She needed release, was desperate for it.

She joined him on the bed and tore off his T-shirt. He was at least semiwilling, raising his arms to help her. But the quizzical look on his face said to her that he was going to start asking questions. And she had no time or inclination for that.

She knelt astride his lap, feeling his hardness between her legs. She hesitated for a second, reveling in the uncertainty on his face. Good—she wanted him to be surprised. Wanted him to understand he didn't know her at all anymore. She threaded her fingers through his short hair and pulled his head back so she could kiss him. She crushed his mouth under hers, needing the force, the pressure to reach the parts inside her that were begging to be released.

She'd never felt so alive, on edge, or desperate for someone before. She wriggled against him, using his dick and the seam of his jeans for friction.

Simon suddenly stood, holding her in place, and turned and deposited her on the bed. He barely looked at her before kicking off his shoes and jeans to stand before her naked. Her eyes devoured the sight of him after all this time. He was slightly more defined, harder than she remembered. But then he probably hadn't been eating at those fancy restaurants in DC like they'd started doing as their wedding had drawn near.

He paused a moment to look at her, splayed out on the bed, and shook his head as if he was trying to clear something from it. *Come on*, she wanted to say, but she didn't want to give him that satisfaction.

He leaned down and ripped open her dress. Buttons pinged and bounced off the surfaces in her small apartment. She knew he could see her tattoo, the one she'd gotten on the day she passed out of The Farm. It was a large vine, growing up the side of her body. She loved it. She'd felt liberated when she'd been accepted to The Farm, like she'd been reaching to the sun, growing in knowledge and ability. He didn't say anything, just ran his fingers over it, sending chills over her skin.

Enough. She wasn't going to take this lying down. She pushed him back with her feet and got up, shucking her bra with no embarrassment and no ceremony. "On the bed," she ordered.

He said nothing, just gave her a wry half smile and grabbed her around the waist, pulling her with him. He tried to take control but she forced him back down. She rubbed her clit against his dick for a few seconds before adjusting her position and sliding him straight inside. She was so wet, had been since she left the meeting earlier. So in need of...something.

Simon groaned as she put her hands on the headboard and rode him. She angled herself so she could go deep, really deep, touching that spot inside her that needed satisfying. She watched the changes on his face as he gazed at her. Disbelief, desire, confusion—it all fed her arousal. Her need for revenge and release.

He slipped his hand between their bodies and for a second touched his dick sliding in and out of her, and then slid his fingers to her clit. She sat up to give him better access, leaning back on her hands so he could see where they were joined. Being in charge of this and being emotionally removed from him gave her such power. Power over herself, power over her feelings, and power over him. He just had no idea. And that turned her on like virtually nothing had before. Like a strong aphrodisiac coursing through her veins.

He withdrew his hand and licked his fingers before running them over her clit, fast, then slow, then building her to her climax as she thrust into him, feeling him from inside out. And as the wave built inside her, rushing over her spine, she gripped the bed covers in her fist and moaned as it peaked and crested over her.

She squeezed his dick as he grabbed her hips and thrust into her, hard and deep. He came, gritting his teeth and almost reluctantly groaning.

They were both out of breath for a moment. And then she needed to be away from him.

What had she done?

You used him to scratch an itch. Like he'd used her for...she wasn't sure what, but she knew that he'd engineered their meeting in Mumbai. And he couldn't know that she knew that. *Shit.*

She avoided his eyes and rolled off him, leaving him. She threw a towel at him from the bathroom and closed the door. There were no clothes for her to wear in there. Damn her for tidying up for once. The other towels were out in the hallway closet, and her robe was by the bed. Good going, Sadie. Just awesome.

She steeled herself and opened the door again. Simon was fastening his jeans with his T-shirt in one hand. He looked up, and she was somewhat gratified to see him check out her body again.

"I sensed that you didn't want me to stick around for cuddling and pillow talk." He shrugged on his T-shirt and picked up the ouzo. "You don't mind? I think I'm going to need this tonight."

"Be my guest," she said evenly.

He hesitated for a second and then opened the door and pointed at the busted lock. "You really should get that looked at," he said as he left.

Had he really gone? She grabbed the towel she'd thrown at him and wrapped it around her as she checked the door. He wasn't in the hallway, so he had actually left. She closed the door with a shaking hand and used the dead bolt to lock it. She would have to get the catch fixed.

She clenched her fists. All the need and frustration and crazy feelings had expired, and now she just felt empty. What had she done?

She pulled on sweatpants and a sweatshirt, despite the heavy heat in the room, and lay on her bed. What was wrong with her? It had been like she'd been possessed. She curled up in a ball, remembering that she'd forgotten to write a report about the meeting but not having the energy to even get her laptop to write it.

Simon. What was he even doing here? Why did he keep appearing at her apartment? Why had he let her use him like that? And why had she?

CHAPTER EIGHT

Simon's morning was not getting off to a good start. He hadn't gotten up with his alarm at five a.m. for his morning run. He hadn't had a protein shake and eggs for breakfast, and he hadn't checked to make sure the finance minister was still in his room.

He'd slept through his alarm and eventually awoke with a headache, the reason for which was lying on its side on the floor next to the bed. How did the Greeks drink that stuff?

Probably because they didn't drink a bottle of it at a time, you stupid ass.

Fuck. This had never happened to him before. He'd never fucked up a mission because of a woman or because of a bottle of alcohol. He took his job far too seriously for that. On occasion he'd gotten rat-assed drunk, but only as part of a job. When he was entertaining a mark.

But when he'd left Sadie's last night, reeling from the hot sex and cold attitude, he dived face-first into the bottle he'd snatched up before he'd left. If he believed in shit like *Mission Impossible*, he'd absolutely have assumed that someone totally different had taken Sadie's face. He'd taken a first gulp of ouzo as he realized that there was nothing left of the Sadie he knew except for her face. Her hair was different, her eyes were cold and angry, her body was harder and—for the love of God—tattooed.

And on top of that, she'd just taken him. Taken him without any emotion, or romance, or cuddling, or anything. He'd left feeling like he could have been just anyone off the street, brought in to scratch an itch. He guessed he should be thankful that she hadn't ordered takeout, or the delivery guy may have had a surprise.

He had no idea what to make of it, so he'd taken another drink, and then another when he remembered how much hate burned in her eyes. He had no idea why. He'd thought fading out of her life completely was what she'd wanted when they called off the wedding. When did she start hating him?

He stepped into the shower to try to drive out the fog in his brain and the smell of aniseed that he was sure was oozing out of his pores. As he stood under the rainfall showerhead, he grabbed a bottle of hotel shampoo before realizing it wasn't. He squinted at the mouthwash label and shrugged. He glugged it right out of the bottle, slooshed, gargled, and spat it at his feet. He felt about 5 percent more human.

What had happened to her? It had been just shy of a year since he'd last seen her, a few days after what was supposed to be their wedding. Somehow in between then and now, something had changed her. Changed her completely. Resolve flooded through him.

He was going to find out what had happened. He was going to fix her. Suddenly invigorated, he finished up his shower and got dressed. He fired up his laptop and checked the microscopic camera he'd installed on the finance minister's floor, directed at his hotel room door. He opened the digital file and replayed it at high speed. No one had left or gone in all night. Indeed, only one room-service guy had walked past the door the whole evening.

He clicked the camera to real time and minimized it so that it was a small square in the corner of his screen. Then he started researching.

Their aborted wedding had been fairly well covered by the media. Sadie's father had managed to minimize the terrorist attempt at hacking into the CIA mainframe and sold it to the media as a dispute between guests at their wedding, which was salacious, but not really newsworthy after a few days.

Sadie had been AWOL from social media for a few months after that. Not that she spent much time online anyway—she usually used it only to keep up with friends from college and her brother and sister-in-law. But there was not even a cute puppy video on her timeline for three and a half months. Then she had posted something cryptic about traveling the world, and the location had been Mumbai. He smiled. That's where he'd met her. Maybe she'd been revisiting everywhere they'd been together, to reclaim those places as hers alone. His sister had done that as a student when her professor boyfriend dumped her for another undergrad. She'd dragged Simon, and sometimes Sadie, to bars and restaurants to "reclaim them" so in her mind they weren't just associated with the professor.

Oh, how he hoped he'd one day bump into the professor. He would crush that dude's head in for hurting his sister. But that was another mission for another day. He really should start keeping a log of the skulls he wanted to smash. At the top of the list would be Platon Asker.

* * *

Sadie was slumped at her desk when Sebastian came in. Her hand was threaded through the handle of a coffee mug, and she hoped her eyes said something like "Don't come too close," or "Handle with care." She suspected he didn't care. Her co-worker was an older man with a sun-lined face and an attitude that came from managing to create a good life for his wife and him despite the covert nature of his job.

She envied him. And she hated herself. The night before had been wonderful. And then horrible. She groaned.

"Too much ouzo last night, or too much something else?" Sebastian said with his characteristic cheeriness.

She just groaned again in response. He grabbed the coffee carafe and sloshed some more into her mug. Some splashed over onto her hand. "Ouch," she said as she jumped and sat upright.

"That's better. I can have a conversation with you now." He looked around at the director's empty office. "This isn't a dorm room. Don't let him catch you lying on your desk like that." He lifted a disapproving eyebrow.

He was right, she knew. She didn't have the luxury of worrying about her own affairs. She sat back in her chair and tucked her hair behind her ears.

Sebastian used his own coffeemaker to make himself a shot of espresso. He had assimilated here. Totally. She watched as he moved about the office, getting his day in order. He'd been at the Athens bureau for over ten years, which was an unheard of length of time for an officer. But he spoke the language like a native, looked like a native, had made firm contacts, and was too valuable an asset to move from the region. Besides which, if they tried, he'd quit. His life was too good here to move away. Sadie wished she felt that way about anywhere in the world. She didn't even know where she could call home anymore.

She flexed her shoulders and turned on her laptop. Enough with the pity party; she had notes to write up. She was supposed to detail every moment of any interaction with anyone not in the agency. But her fingers hesitated on Simon. She didn't want to admit her postoperation weakness last night, and she didn't want to necessarily inform anyone that her ex-fiancé was in town. Especially since she still didn't know why he was here. Official or unofficial.

She typed everything up on her contact sheet and then cut and pasted the parts about Simon into a different file.

At The Farm they'd emphasized over and over again that every single contact with a local had to be documented. Whether it was the old woman in the bodega where she bought newspapers and gum or a waiter she'd chatted to while picking up a salad for lunch.

She'd started wondering if it was some kind of ploy to keep their field officers sitting at their desk for the majority of their time, when Sebastian had taken her for lunch and explained that everyone had two sets of reports. One for the boss, to include waiters, shopkeepers, and marks. And one for her other colleagues that had the stuff you didn't necessarily want the director to see. They swapped passwords and made a pact not to open the documents unless someone was in trouble or uncontactable.

It seemed to work. She'd put a trigger warning on her file, so she knew no one in the office had opened it in the months she'd been there. Not that there was much to put in it up to now. A minor flirtation with one of the marines at the US embassy and more recently about kissing Platon. But today, of course, Simon was being sent to the unofficial report file too.

As she wrote about his visit to her apartment, a flush started at her chest until she could feel it heating up her neck and face. She grabbed a thin scarf she had on the back of her chair and wrapped it around her, hoping Sebastian hadn't seen the blush. Luckily he was the only one in the office. Sometimes she didn't see the others for weeks at a time. The other two men were sent farther out into Macedonia and Albania from the Athens office. Sadie suspected that one day she'd also be sent out beyond Athens. Which made her remember to fill out the paperwork she'd been putting off to take the Greek language course the office paid for.

"So what happened last night to make you so despondent this morning and so hot when you wrote your report?" Sebastian said as he got up for another cup of coffee.

Damn, of course he'd seen. She should've known he'd pick

up on every detail; it was part of what made him so good at his job. Sadie liked Sebastian, and his Greek wife, Netta. If there was anyone in the whole of Athens she could tell, it would be him. But she hesitated. She was excellent at keeping secrets, with a father who was the director of the CIA and a brother whose professional exploits she'd managed to keep from her family for years. Excellent at lying.

"Do you really want to know?" she asked with a deliberate playfulness in her eyes. "I mean, can your heart take it, old man?" She laughed at the expression of mock outrage on his face. "Give me one of your exquisite coffees and I'll tell you."

He laughed and made her some of his thick espresso, even going so far as to grab a lemon from the old fridge and peel a tiny curl of zest from it, placing it carefully on the rim of the tiny cup.

She smiled in delight. "Okay. Last night I met my mark and we went dancing. We drank a little, he talked—*a lot*—and we danced until the early hours. And then I may have gotten entirely inappropriate with him."

Sebastian's eyebrows shot up into his unruly, curly salt-and-pepper hair.

"We kissed and danced, and oh my God, he was so sweet and *so* young." She cast her eyes to the ceiling as if she were remembering the encounter and smiled.

"Good for you, darling. How old is he again?"

"Twenty-two," she whispered, grinning.

"Ahhh, I remember that age. So hopeful, so eager. I hope it wasn't all over in twenty seconds. I remember that part too," he said, shaking his head.

She was amazed that he seemed to be completely okay with her sleeping with a mark. At The Farm, they'd always been told to avoid emotional entanglements, but they'd never specifically mentioned physical ones, and at the time she'd wondered if they didn't want to actively encourage or discourage anyone from taking that last step to get the job done.

Somehow it was fine for James Bond to sleep with any woman to get his mission completed, but for women she'd wondered if the same held true. Certainly Sebastian didn't seem fazed by the thought that she might have slept with Platon. Maybe she shouldn't be fazed by it either.

"Just be careful he doesn't get attached to you," Sebastian said, cocking his head.

"What do you mean? I thought the idea was for them to get attached." She put down her cup and frowned over her laptop at him. She realized now that it was way too hot for the scarf and took it off again. Despite the fans in the office, it was still blisteringly hot. Good thing she liked the heat.

"Attached, but not too attached. The problem with some of the people we need to...*befriend* in our line of business is that they are not always completely normal. Maybe they already know they are in danger; maybe they are living a double life and are trying to juggle too many things. It makes them both vulnerable and slightly unpredictable. Don't trust anyone." He shrugged and went back to his own PC.

She knew very well that what he was saying was true. She sometimes got the impression that Platon felt slightly out of his depth. Occasionally he was distracted or a little sharp with his words. She tried her best to soothe him when he was on edge and hoped that she would never have to reveal who she was and how deeply he'd gotten himself in trouble. Because even though he didn't understand it right now, he would be in a whole shit storm of trouble if Stratigos ever found out he'd brought a CIA officer into their meeting. Anarchists did not mess around when it came to revenge or betrayal. Car bombs were business as usual for them. As sweet as Platon was, he hung out with terrorists and was probably involved in something bad. It did her no favors to like him and feel sympathy for him. She needed to remind herself of that.

And Sebastian was right about not trusting anyone. All the people she knew here, including the director and Sebastian, were expert liars. Even she was. She hadn't told anyone that she'd taken the thumb drive back from the director's desk and wouldn't. When she was in the DOD, there was a firm reporting structure. Someone had always known what she was doing and where she was. Hell, the things she did were written into her performance appraisal. Being a field officer was totally different. Even though they had a station chief—for what Lassiter was worth—they'd been taught to keep everything they did quiet until it yielded results. Deniability at all costs, maybe. But autonomy was the name of the game in fieldwork.

Regardless of the appearance of glamour, working in the CIA was lonely. Really lonely.

* * *

Her day was spent, as most usually were, going through candid photos of people who fellow officers around Europe had identified as being "of interest" for one reason or another. She had been taught to absorb the photos and tuck them away so she would recognize them if she came across them.

As she grabbed her bag and shut down her computer for the day, a phone in the office rang. Sebastian met her eyes. She shook her head; she had no idea who was calling. Four companies had "offices" in their suite and each had a separate phone number.

Sebastian picked up the line. "Devries Construction, please hold." He pressed the HOLD button. "Did you give someone your number?" he asked.

"Of course I didn't. It's either a marketing call or..." She bit her lip, wondering if Stratigos was testing her.

Sebastian tipped his head to one side and shook it slightly. He looked disappointed in her, but she wasn't ready to tell anyone about her op, because until she had at least a plot or a target to be concerned about, all she had was conjecture. And rookie humiliation.

"Devries Construction. Thank you for holding. How may I direct your call?" He paused and then his eyes met hers again, lips tightening. "Absolutely; let me put you through." He pressed HOLD and said calmly, "Line one for you."

She picked up her phone and sat back down, swiveling away from Sebastian's look. She put on a bored voice. "Inventory Management, Sadie speaking."

There was rustling and muffled voices in the background, and then, "Sadie?" It was Platon.

"Platon? Why did you call my work number? If my boss were here, you could have gotten me in trouble," she half whispered.

Another muffled conversation. "I tried to get you on your cell phone, but you didn't pick up. I had a gap between shifts and wondered if you wanted to grab a beer before I have to go back to the hotel."

Sadie turned over her cell phone. Five bars of signal and zero missed calls. Stratigos was testing her. He'd dialed and then handed the phone to Platon. She could see them in her mind's eye, Platon's panic about why he was calling, Stratigos giving him the answers and telling him what to say.

Excitement spiked through her. "Sure. I was just leaving work. Shall we meet at the Athinas in the Plaka?" She knew this was walking distance from the hotel he worked at and far enough away from her apartment so he couldn't suggest anything untoward.

"Perfect. I will see you there in twenty minutes."

"See you!" she replied cheerfully before hanging up.

"Do I want to know?" Sebastian asked as he took his empty coffee cup to the kitchen. She knew he was being supportive, but she also knew that he really *didn't* want to know what her operation was about. Sharing operational information, other than in their report files, was frowned upon. At The Farm, they'd explained that it was an important security measure: If things went south and an officer was captured or interrogated—or worse—then he would only know about his own op and no one else's.

"Not yet. It's early days," she replied. "Probably nothing."

"Be careful out there, darling," he said from inside the kitchen.

CHAPTER NINE

Simon's finance minister had actually been working that day, instead of skipping around town meeting girlfriends and socialites. He was a good-looking man, one who stuck out like a sore thumb in the Russian cabinet. All the other members were gray haired and old, and he was in his late thirties and had a thick head of dark hair.

Minister Stamov was the only one young enough to not remember the "old days" of Mother Russia. Usually the younger generation in Russia came out against the president's reign... but given that any intel from Russia was hard to come by these days, he couldn't be sure about anything.

It wasn't CAG's job to think about the politics behind a mission. Once you tried to overthink it or believed you had information that someone else didn't, you were usually fucked.

Anyway, as far as Simon could tell, Stamov seemed to have enjoyed the day of banking meetings that he'd been attending.

He was in the lobby, watching the minister rotate around groups of suited men and women, all clutching cocktails that few seemed to be enjoying.

A man sat down in an armchair opposite Simon. He was tall, Western, early thirties or maybe in his twenties with some miles on his face. The battered cowboy boots didn't tell him much, and his shirt...

"Hey, mate. Dog can't fly without umbrella," the man said in a British accent, grinning widely.

Simon bristled. What the fuck was he talking about? He sat up and looked around to see if anyone was watching.

"Oh, don't get your knickers in a twist; I was sent by..." He looked to the ceiling and wrinkled his nose as if he was trying to recall. "Ringling? No, Barnum. Is that right? What a name, right? I wonder if his boss ever says, 'Are you running a circus here, Goddamnit?'" He'd assumed a pretty good American accent for the last bit. But Simon only barely noticed it.

This guy was insane, and he had to get away from him before his cover was blown. He folded his newspaper, but as he put it down and made to leave, the man grinned. "Sit down, mate. Don't be a twat. I'm just messing with you." Simon hesitated but watched, intrigued, as the man held up his hand and asked a waiter to bring them both scotch and sodas, affecting a really impressive French accent.

"I wanted some kind of ridiculous password to give you, like they do in the movies, but they didn't give me one." He shrugged. "Your people are no fun, mate."

"You can stop calling me 'mate,' for a start."

"See? No fun." He turned to receive his drinks from the

waiter, tossed a twenty-euro note on his silver tray, and said, "*Merci beaucoup, mon ami.*"

Simon wanted to hit him. He wasn't sure why; he just really wanted to hit him. "So who are you, and keep your fucking voice down this time."

"Mal Garrett. My friends call me Mal; you can call me Garrett." He paused to give Simon an insincere smile. "I work private. But my boss used to serve with yours and blah, blah, blah. Long story short, he sent me to pick up your slack. There's been a problem getting your boys in country. I'm just filling in until they do. So I guess I'm your temp." He took a healthy swig of his drink and sat back in the armchair and looked around at the lobby. "Jesus, I can't believe I'm back here again. I was here a couple of weeks ago, sent out on a babysitting mission, and now I'm dragged back here for a few days. Eh, at least the booze is good."

Jesus Christ, did the dude ever stop talking? But then again, it was becoming difficult watching and following Stamov alone, not to mention keeping an eye on Sadie and her new boyfriend. "Come upstairs; I have his schedule and his car license plate and..."

"No need, Tennant. I already have my brief." He threw a cell phone at Simon, who caught it without taking his eyes off Garrett's. "You can get me on that if you need me. I'm going to unpack and then I'll be all over Stamov like a rash. No sweat." His eyes flickered over Simon's shoulder. "Or maybe you can just take the evening off."

At that second, he stood up as the finance minister held out his hand. "Fran?ois! I didn't know you would be here."

Simon backed away fast as Garrett scoffed at the minister's proffered hand and instead brought Stamov into a Gallic embrace. "It is so good to see you, my friend. I only agreed to come because of the fine cellar of wine they keep at the hotel here. You must join me to take advantage of it, *oui*?"

"But of course, comrade. Already you have made this visit more pleasurable. Come. Let us leave this party and"—his voice rose in excitement—"make our own party!" Some of the minister's hangers-on applauded and cheered.

Simon had seen nothing like it in his life. Garrett must have been on the job for a long time to achieve that level of comfort with a Russian cabinet member. What the hell was his background that he could seamlessly switch between characters? He wondered if he was even English.

Anyway, as soon as he could get upstairs and check out Garrett's story, Simon knew exactly how he was going to spend his unexpectedly free evening.

It took three minutes on the phone to Barnum to confirm his new "partner" was legit. His boss promised to send the unredacted parts of Garrett's file if he could get his hands on it but assured him that he was the best available backup.

Simon was worried, however, that his team was having issues getting into Greece, but his boss told him it was need to know, and he didn't. Business as usual at CAG. He signed off and pulled up the phone app that let him find Sadie. He'd stuck a microscopic chip into her purse when she'd gone to the bathroom. It was done on pure instinct. He always kept at least ten of the trackers in his wallet because you never knew when you were going to lose a mark. If one went into a busy subway station, by far the best bet at continuing surveillance was to tag the mark and then just wait for him to materialize again. He just hadn't gotten close enough to put one on the minister yet, but since Garrett and he were such good friends, maybe he'd delegate that job.

Since he'd sneaked it into her bag, he'd justified it a million times in his head by telling himself that it was for her safety. He owed her at least safety while he was in the city. It was a gift that she wouldn't know she'd received.

It sounded weak even to him.

* * *

Sadie managed to snag their favorite table outside the Athinas bar and café. It was important for Platon to feel comfortable whenever he was with her, and these little things built up trust, whether he knew it or not.

And of course he never would.

She ordered a coffee so that she could order them both a beer when he arrived without overdoing it. As she looked around for him, she took out a notepad and pen to scribble down a shopping list. Again, totally nonthreatening. Something that a mom would do. Her whole time with Platon was built around these layers of security and comfort. Every time she met him she was careful to give him absolutely nothing to question later. She even tucked her cell phone out of sight so he didn't suspect she was recording him. If she was 100 percent right about him, his paranoia would slowly be growing.

Also, she really needed to get some groceries. Milk, coffee, bread. She tapped the pen against her teeth as she watched people walk by. Salad, carrots, soda. The chair next to her scraped out and she looked up with a big smile that stayed on her face for less than a second.

"Simon. What the fuck?" She looked around to see if anyone was watching them. "You have to go. I'm expecting someone." Goddamn him. She swore if the waiter had left the silverware that had been wrapped in a napkin on the table, she'd be holding the knife to his jugular.

"What's the matter? You think your boyfriend won't want to see me? Won't want to know what we did last night?" He looked around, as if searching for a waiter to order a drink.

She decided on a play. Not perfect, but it would do the job for now. She lowered her voice. "Look, please go. He's a sweet boy, but he's going to get super jealous if he sees you." She cast her eyes down slowly as if she couldn't bear to meet his eyes. "I know I did a"—pause, swallow—"terrible thing last night, and I'm really sorry. But please don't get me in trouble with my boyfriend." She slid her gaze back up to his.

Concern was etched on his face, and his eyes searched hers for the truth, but he obviously found no reason to disbelieve her.

Inside she celebrated. Outside, she bit her lip and frowned very lightly.

"I'll leave now if you promise to meet me later," he said, getting up.

"Anything. Absolutely," she replied, relief gushing through her.

"This restaurant at eight." He handed her the type of card

you pick up at a hotel from one of those wooden dispensers near the elevators.

"Eight. Okay. It's a—" She hesitated.

He swooped down, blocking out the sun, and kissed her. Heat rose inside. It was over before it had begun, but his lips seared her skin. "Yeah. It is," he said as he left.

She watched as he wove between the tables and away from the restaurant. Her heartbeat steadied, and she looked again for Platon. No sign of him. She went back to her shopping list but didn't even see the words. That had been terrifying. But the kiss...She shook that out of her mind and concentrated on the important outrage. Weeks of work could have been flushed down the toilet, not to mention the fact that there was a chance that she was mere steps away from cracking an awful scheme. She steadied her breath and counted the number of taps she made on the paper with her pen. Counting was soothing for her.

Eventually she added eggs to the list, just as Platon arrived. He'd obviously been running. She smiled.

"I am so sorry to be late," he said in his charming English.

"I forgive you," she said, grinning and turning up her face so he could kiss her. His kiss smelled of sun and fresh air. Why wasn't he just an ordinary, fun guy who could help her take her mind—and anger—away from Simon?

He sat and made some special Greek sign for beers. Maybe they just knew him. The one time she'd tried it, the waiter had brought her a menu instead of a beer. "What are you doing, *koukla mou*?" he asked as he laid an arm along the back of his chair.

"Just making a shopping list. My apartment is virtually empty of food!" she said. "I think I have a tomato and an old piece of cheese."

He laughed, as she'd meant him to. "I can't believe I still haven't seen your apartment after all this time," he said with a lazy smile that anyone would interpret as a come-on.

"You'll get to see it...eventually." She winked at him and he laughed again.

"You are lucky I have so many things to do all the time or I'm sure I'd follow you home and make you show me," he said.

The waiter arrived with their tall glasses of heavily frothed, cold beer. She hoped that was just an expression and that he didn't make a habit of following girls home and forcing his way into their homes. She took a sip to cover the expression that could have flickered across her face if she hadn't been on guard. Maybe it was just...nope; she couldn't believe someone would say that without knowing exactly what he was inferring. He was getting more confident, or at least pushier, and she wondered why. Thank goodness she wasn't just an average girl on the street. She could certainly handle him if push came to shove, but she needed to postpone that moment as long as possible.

"You know I'm not...you know. I like to take my time..." She closed her eyes as if she were embarrassed, and laughed awkwardly.

"You are beautiful and innocent. A perfect combination."

She sat up straight as if pleased with his compliment and giggled into her drink. She moved the conversation on to his family and his work at the hotel and kept it light. He wasn't bad company when they were just chitchatting.

But while they sat in the sun, her mind flickered to dinner with Simon. She couldn't just not show up and just hope that she didn't run into him again. He'd just track her down again, and her luck might not hold out next time.

When Platon got up to return to work, she kissed him, hoping to find that anyone could arouse the kind of heat Simon had raised in her. But no. She felt nothing. *Damn Simon.*

Damn Simon. Damn him all to hell. She checked her watch as she was walking back to her apartment. She had an hour to get ready. An hour-ish. She didn't really care if she was late—let him sit there and fret about whether she was coming or not.

She felt sticky, and she could still smell Platon's aftershave on her. She'd just shower and change clothes.

And put on some fresh makeup and a little perfume. And remind Simon of what he'd refused to fight for.

Shit. Why did she even care what he thought? She refused to answer that question as she stepped into her apartment and got in the shower to wash the day away.

CHAPTER TEN

Simon sat at a table in the restaurant he'd picked from a rack of cards at the concierge desk. It was far enough away from his hotel and her apartment that he wouldn't be tempted to...he didn't know what. It would be a toss-up between dragging her back to either place to duct tape her to the wall to keep her safe from her "boyfriend," or dragging her back and doing all kinds of other things with this new Sadie.

He'd been sure that the routine she'd given at the café was in some way insincere, but with him not seeming to be able to get a bead on this new Sadie, he couldn't tell for certain.

Maybe she had gotten in over her head with Asker. Maybe she was just appealing to the part of him that still cared about her. He was all switched around and upside down, and he didn't much care for the feeling. He hadn't felt unsure about anything for years. It just wasn't in his nature. But she was so hard to read. Yes, he should walk away, but he couldn't. He needed to know why she had changed so dramatically. And what the previous night had been about.

He shifted in his seat uncomfortably at the thought of the sex they'd had. It had been horrible and fascinating and hot as hell all at once. She'd treated him like a fucking man-whore, used him, and immediately went cold. Shit, he couldn't even remember if they'd kissed. She'd turned him into Julia fucking Roberts.

Sadie was ten minutes late. When she appeared at the maître d's desk, she just pointed at Simon's table and snaked her way through the other diners toward him. She looked happy and relaxed, which he wasn't expecting. And really fucking hot. Her slightly tanned skin shimmered in the dim light of the restaurant, and her short, just-fell-out-of-bed hair belied her determined eyes. She looked casual, but it was easy to see that she had purpose. He tipped his head slightly in contemplation. He'd never noticed this much about her before. It was as if she'd suddenly come into sharp contrast before him.

She wore a dress with small cutouts that revealed skin on either side of her waist. The short skirt was flared and had layers of thin material that made him want to see what they were hiding. He knew what was under there, but the dress was doing terrible things to his brain. And dick.

"I wasn't sure if you'd come," he said, rising to pull out her chair.

"Why?" she replied with a smile.

"Because...I feel as if I don't know the first thing about you anymore," he said honestly.

"Maybe you never knew me as well as you thought. Did you

consider that?" she asked, sitting back in her chair.

He gave her a small smile as he sat back into his seat. "It felt like I knew you very well."

"Things aren't always as they seem." She nodded at the waiter, who had grabbed the wine from the silver wine bucket next to the table.

What was that supposed to mean?

"Your father told me you left the DoD. What made you do that?"

A flash in her eyes. What was that? Fear? Surprise? God-damnit—why couldn't he get a handle on her?

"You spoke to my father? When?"

"A few months ago. A business call," he lied.

She paused, watching his face.

"Why?" She took a sip of wine. Her eyes fluttered shut for a second as she tasted it. He'd picked an expensive wine that she'd cooed over at a wine tasting back in DC. So maybe Sadie hadn't completely changed.

"It was a work-related thing."

"If you've only brought me here to lie, I think I'm done." She put her napkin by the side of her plate and slid her chair out.

Shit.

He put his hand lightly on her arm. "Okay, I spoke to him this morning. I'm sorry. I didn't want to piss you off even more."

She sat and smiled. "See? Telling the truth isn't *that* hard. So let's try again, and don't forget I have a built-in bullshit detector when it comes to you. Why did you call my father?"

What the hell was she talking about? "I told him that I'd seen you here and that you were in the company of someone...we know."

"*We* know?" she asked, interest sparking in her eyes.

Maybe she *would* pay attention to this. "He's associated with some bad people."

"Associated how?" she asked, leaning forward slightly.

"He's been photographed with several Greek persons of interest." There. That should do it. She'd always respected his job and his—

She burst out laughing. "This is Athens, Simon. Everyone knows everyone. If you take enough photos, I'm sure you'd find me standing next to all manner of 'persons of interest.'" She laughed again, holding her napkin briefly to her lips as if she was scared she'd make too much noise. She took another sip of wine. "Look. Athens is like DC. So many crooks masquerading as regular people, and so many regular people masquerading as crooks."

It was good to see her laugh. Properly laugh. He sat back and did the same. "I suppose you're right. Man, DC—I'm not sad to be away from that scene. Don't get me wrong: I'd have stood by your side at those cocktail parties my whole life for you. But sometimes it was like swimming for your life in a shallow pool filled with sharks and piranhas."

Her eyes softened. "I had no idea you hated it so much. If it's any consolation, I wasn't keen myself. But it was always hard to say no to Mother. You remember."

He laughed again. "Oh yes; I do remember. We were that close to eloping before she guilt-tripped us into staying for the big wedding." He took a swig of wine. "That close." He held up his fingers a millimeter apart.

A pained look flashed across her face and she leaned forward. "I'm so sorry about that. I had no idea..."

"No. How could you know that our wedding would descend into something out of *Apocalypse Now*?"

"That's not what I meant. I'm sorry that you spent a year doing things you didn't want to do because of me." She frowned. "I never realized, and I should have."

"What are you...No, that's not what I meant. I just wanted to be with you. As long as you were there, I would have been happy anywhere. A cocktail party, a war zone, or I don't know...spending time with your family?" He deliberately made it sound worse than being in a war zone to make her smile. It worked.

"I know. Talk about above and beyond the call of duty. Sometimes I wonder if it would have just been easier if we'd faked our own deaths and gone to live on a desert island somewhere."

"Eh. I already thought that one through. Your father would have found us."

She laughed again. "Yes, he would have. No doubt about it. Remember when..." Her voice trailed off.

"Yes, I do. I *do* remember when he LoJacked your car to make sure we were on our way to the Smithsonian benefit and not having a Five Guys burger in Alexandria," Simon said, wanting somehow to make her remember. To see the old Sadie.

He felt like there was some kind of veil between them...like camo netting. He could see her, but he couldn't really *see* her. Couldn't reach the Sadie he had known.

He poured some more wine into her glass and paused the conversation as they gave their orders to the waiter.

"What's been going on since I last saw you?" he asked casually as if he desperately didn't want to know every last detail.

She took a sip of the icy wine and then licked the tip of her finger where moisture from the glass must have been. "After you disappeared, I quit my job, cut my hair...all those stereotypical things that we girls are supposed to do in the face of a breakup." She stopped talking to take another sip.

He resisted the temptation to explain or apologize. He let the silence sit there.

"And I came here. Took an English-speaking job so I could afford a kebab and some wine every now and again, and started dating. What about you?"

He paused. It all seemed so logical, and yet his instinct told him something was wrong. All wrong. God, he wanted to shake her until the truth rattled out. But he wondered if he'd recognize the truth even if he got at it.

She was beginning to piss him off.

* * *

She wanted to have fun with him, like they used to. To banter back and forth, make light of the problems they faced with jokes and jibes.

He looked so good, sitting across the table from her as he'd done so many times before. Strong tan arms, with muscles that flexed just under the skin whenever he moved, short sandy hair—longer than the usual military style—that she used to run her fingers through when he kissed her, and intently blue eyes that were slow to smile...but when they did...She remembered the joy she felt when something she said creased his strong jaw and solemn face into a smile or even a laugh. What had happened to the two of them?

But she couldn't afford to mess this operation up or lose her job because she accidentally told someone what she did. And that included Simon. Oh sure, they were working for the same government, but she wasn't naive enough to think they always went about things from the same perspective or with the same goals. In fact, some of the biggest intelligence blowbacks had come precisely because of that gaping chasm between agencies. But it wasn't her job to fix that by breaking her oath as a CIA officer.

And of course, if she slipped up, let something out that she shouldn't, hinted at something, then Simon would be duty bound to report it to his superiors. So she was saving him from that decision too.

None of that changed one thing, though: She still wanted him. In all honesty, she could've made do just fine with her favorite vibrator that night she'd been so high off infiltrating Platon's meeting. She hadn't slept with Simon just because he'd happened to show up. She'd jumped on him because she'd wanted to feel that familiarity, that closeness with him. She'd missed it. She'd missed being able to turn to him for advice during her training. And yesterday, she'd tried to reconnect with that, but on her terms.

"How long are you in town for?" she asked, breaking the silence that he'd left hanging over the table, presumably in the attempt to have her fill it with more details about her life.

"I'm not sure. And I don't care; I have the nicest hotel room I think the government has ever given me." He smiled and continued eating.

"What have you been doing since you got here?" she pressed on.

"Just looking around. What do you suggest I do?" She could have sworn he sighed.

"Well, the Acropolis, of course. The museum of archaeology is a great place too."

He wiped his mouth with his napkin and threw it on the table. "Okay, we have to stop this. I'm frankly terrified that you're going to get up and disappear without us talking about something real. Like your young boyfriend. Like the danger you seem oblivious to. Like what the hell happened last night. And what the hell happened to you in this past year."

She started at his vehemence and was forced to put a hand on his arm and look around to indicate to him that people were listening to his raised voice.

"Simon. What's the matter with you?" She could see him flexing his fists in his lap, so she knew he was trying to get a handle on this inappropriate anger.

An anger that was making her really wonder why he was really here and what was going on. Was he on a similar op?

"Okay; let's get out of here and talk where we won't be disturbing anyone else's dinner," she said.

He threw way too many notes on the table, clamped his hand around her arm, and led her out onto the street. She could have gotten his hand off her in a second, but that would only expose her training, and she had to keep that buried around him. "Get your hand off me," she hissed.

"No fucking way, princess. I'm still not sure you won't make a run for it." But he did loosen his grip a little.

The streets were busy and noisy with people, which is pretty much what she loved most about Athens. It was kind of like New York in the number of people who stayed out partying all night.

He led her to a small street garden—a patch of grass with benches, where an ancient building used to be. Old ruined walls added to the seclusion and atmosphere of the place.

"Start talking," he said, shoving her onto one of the benches and sitting.

"All of those things you asked—everything you want to know—are none of your business now. We're not friends. You made sure of that when you disappeared." And when she'd realized she'd been his mark in Mumbai.

His jaw tightened in the moonlight. "So what was last night? You can fuck me, but we're still not friends?"

Ah, shit. She looked away and gazed into the darkness of the park. "That was nothing. A mistake," she said firmly, still not managing to meet his eyes.

She jumped as his fingers clasped her chin and made her look at him.

"We might not be friends, Sadie. But we are something."

She moved her head so that he let go of her chin. "You used to tell me that I was your everything. Your port in a storm. Your sanctuary when you came back from a mission. Did you ever wonder what you were to me? You were the man who always disappeared. The man who was there but only until your phone rang. I loved you, but you were a ghost to me. Is that the 'something' you mean?"

"Sadie." He looked devastated, and she cursed herself for saying those things. As true as they were, she hadn't wanted to explore their relationship right then. Nor ever, if truth be told.

She lightened her expression. "But that's all just history, isn't it?"

He leaned in. She knew he meant to kiss her, and she wanted to move, wanted to slap his face and run. That's what she should have done.

Instead she allowed her mouth to open slightly as her eyes fluttered closed. Just one kiss. A safe good-bye kiss...and then all rational thought escaped her.

His tongue touched hers and her senses and nerve endings came alive. He felt like home. A dark, impenetrable, warm, and sexy home. Her heartbeat raced and butterflies heralded the coming of spring in her stomach. He still wanted her. She still wanted him. She didn't care about anything else.

She held his face as she stood and climbed astride his thighs, still kissing him. His hands went to her breasts, and he ran the backs of them over the swell above her neckline. And then he found the zipper of the dress and pulled it down to her waist.

He yanked her toward him and put his mouth around her nipples, through her bra. As he sucked and bit, she arched her back, aching for him to make her feel more. And more.

She grabbed his short hair and rammed her mouth against his. She wanted to hurt him, to be hurt by him, to bruise her mouth, so she'd be sure his being here wasn't some crazy fucked-up illusion. But mostly so he'd regret lying to her and leaving her.

His dick strained against his cargo pants, and she ground herself against it, moving her hips so that she could feel the whole length of him.

"Stop," he whispered, out of breath. "Not like this. I don't want to hurt you."

"Now you decide you don't want to hurt me?" she whispered back, not wanting to lose the moment. She wanted to come so badly.

His hand splayed against her throat, dragging his fingers slowly from her chin to her bra. His mouth followed, slow and firm. She wanted to protest, but his tongue snaked a hot trail over her pulse points, making her heart race. She'd protest in a minute.

"You've changed so much," he murmured against her throat.

She was about to respond when he found his way under her skirt to her panties. He slipped under them as if he was trained in stealth. Which he was.

For a second she was embarrassed at how wet she was for him. But the new Sadie took over and moaned as his fingers slid against her gently. She'd forgotten how the slightest touch from Simon would have her climbing the heights of pleasure. How had she forgotten that?

She arched again, this time rising from her knees to allow him better access. He pressed against her clit with his thumb as he slid a finger inside her. Heat spread through her, and she gasped for air. It wasn't enough; it just wasn't enough. She wanted to feel him all over, wanted him naked and hard all over beneath her fingers. She wanted to touch him in a way that she never had before. This wasn't the place for that.

Neither of them could afford the scrutiny if the police happened to wander in to the quiet gardens. "We...shouldn't do this here..." she said, voice cracking.

"I don't care. Do you care?"

"If you get caught..."

"I won't get caught," he whispered. "But if it makes you feel better, I absolutely won't tell anyone that you jumped me as I was taking my evening walk."

She laughed and was about to retort that no one would believe he'd be that lucky, when he grabbed her hips and stood with her legs around his waist. He strode toward a half-tumbled-down wall. Actually a T section of wall covered in graffiti to within an inch of its life. He set her down and pushed her back into the angle of the wall. They were completely invisible now.

Her pulse picked up again as he tore off his shirt over his head. Her fingers trailed a damp path down his chest. His own hands stayed at his side, fists clenched. Why wasn't he touching her?

"Tell me what you're doing here, Sadie."

Did he mean here here, or in Athens? There was no way he was going to interrogate her

while she was standing here in her bra.

"I'm trying to fuck my ex out of my head," she said, knowing her words would shock him. She reached behind her and removed her bra. A muscle clenched in his jaw. *Score.*

He still didn't move. So she turned around and, bending at the waist, shimmied out of her panties. When they were on the ground, she braced herself against the wall with her arms. "Do I have to remind you what to do? I can recommend a sex-ed boo—"

The noise of the slap reached her faster than the sharp pain on her butt. She gasped and tried to turn around. He wouldn't let her.

"Enough. You stay right there, missy." He put her hands back on the wall and kicked her feet apart. "You've been...bad. Very, very bad. You fuck me like I'm some gigolo, you refuse to tell me anything that's going on in your life, you have a boyfriend—in case you've forgotten—and now you try to distract me. Am I wrong?"

She had no comeback. She was about to accuse him of desertion the previous year, when he flipped up her dress's skirt around her waist. Words choked in her throat as his fingers lightly scraped down her butt to the top of her thighs. A thread of something lit up in her. A pulse of life. She couldn't help but bend over a little more.

He just laughed and slid his hand between her legs. "Jesus. You're so wet. Is that for me or for your boyfriend?" He was brutal.

She moaned. She wanted to dive into this feeling, this moment, and never come up again.

He slipped a finger inside her and she groaned. "Do you want me to fuck you?"

He'd never used that word before when they'd been in bed.

She suspected he was trying to turn her on and make her feel bad. It was working. It was so fucked up.

"Yes," she gasped over her shoulder. She felt like everything inside her would come tumbling out if he didn't.

He spanked her again and spun her around. "I'm going to fuck you all right, but you are going to be facing me, not turning away, imagining it's someone else inside you. You're going to know for sure it's me."

He undid his pants with one hand. The parts of his body she could see in the dim light were a work of art, as they always had been, all defined muscles and swagger, but she had no time to look at it. He grabbed her butt and dragged her to him, lifting her so that she had to wrap her legs around him.

He backed her into the wall and, with one hand, took his dick and thrust into her. Her back grazed against the wall, adding friction and pain to the pleasure that was pulsing through her.

He stayed there, not moving. She tightened her muscles around him. *Come on. I need this.*

He pulled her hair down her back, exposing her neck to him again. Biting down on her throat gently, he groaned and started sliding in and out of her, each thrust taking him farther and farther into her. She felt as if she were absorbing him.

She rocked her hips, needing all of him to fill her up. "More," she whispered, as he moved his head to look at her. She lowered her mouth to his and kissed him, softly at first, almost like a declaration of love. His tongue pushed against hers, as if he couldn't get enough of her, and the kiss became deeper. His thrusts became more forceful and faster. Heat expanded in her as he tore his mouth away from hers and groaned as he came. She rocked her hips lightly against him, reveling for a second in the power she had over him like this.

When they were just talking, she was on guard, flippant, playing a role. With Simon buried deep inside her, losing himself in her, she was free from all that. Free from everything. It was a strangely addicting feeling. One that had her hypersensitive to everything, as if every cell on her body had a cool breeze blowing on it, even in this sticky, still, humid heat.

Simon put her down slowly and then stretched his arms out on either side of her on the wall. He took a breath.

Sadie was worried he was about to get serious again. "That'll be sixty euros, mister," she said with wide eyes.

He drew his head up and peered down at her.

"What? You're the one who brought up hookers." She winked at him cheekily and he burst out laughing.

"You're the worst."

"Yes, I am." She bent over to get her bra and picked up his shirt too. Pushing it into his stomach, she said, "You should get dressed. You look like the Terminator. No sense startling the locals."

He laughed again and shook his head. "Jesus, Sadie. I can't believe how much you've changed. It's like...I don't know. Were you holding back with me before? Were you...scared of me or something?"

Her heart dropped. She didn't mean for him to think that what they had wasn't real. Or...*but wait*. He lied to her when he met her. She had to remember that. She'd been thinking about it constantly since she left The Farm, and yet after just a couple of nights with Simon, it had somehow slipped out of the front of her mind.

"What? No," she scoffed. "I've just had...different experiences since we broke up. Learned more about myself." Shit, what was she saying? She meant she'd become more independent and empowered, but as she said the words she realized that it had sounded like she'd been spending her time sleeping with guys.

His eyes narrowed and he looked away as he put on his shirt. "Come on. I'll walk you back to your apartment."

"There's no need," she said, struggling into her panties and stuffing her bra in her purse. His voice was suddenly hard, and every part of her wanted to reassure him that she wasn't sleeping around, but her brain told her that she didn't need to. It wasn't on her to clear up any confusion he had about her life. It was nothing to do with him.

"I'm going to take you anyway."

"What if I don't want to go to my apartment?" she asked, ire rising.

He stopped and stared at her for a moment. "Whatever." He turned and walked away, through the garden, disappearing from view almost immediately—something she thought she was used to.

It still hurt.

CHAPTER ELEVEN

He'd followed her home—of course he had. There was no way he was going to let her walk home by herself with that glow on her face and her bra in her bag. She'd gone straight back to her apartment, not even noticing the number of men who'd walked past her and craned their necks looking at her when she passed. He'd wanted to snap their necks for just looking, but he pushed away those emotions and concentrated on the mission: Get Sadie home safely.

He'd loitered on the opposite side of the road as she went in. He saw her light go on but only left some minutes later when the light was finally extinguished.

Bars called out to him like a siren song, but as much as he wanted to drown in some liquor somewhere, he knew he couldn't fuck up like that two nights in a row. He needed some sleep.

He walked past the hotel bar on his way to his room and clocked Garrett and the minister still awake, giggling—there was really no other word for it—over the small table they were sitting at. The minister's minders stood around the wall. When Mal saw him, his face evened out for a split second, giving a virtually imperceptible nod. He then started laughing again at something the minister said. Clearly Simon had made the right choice by not drinking. They couldn't both have a hangover tomorrow.

He went to his room and stepped into the shower before lying naked in the dark, wondering what the hell was going on with Sadie.

* * *

"Get your cacks on, mate. I don't need to see that." Something hit him in the face, and he sat bolt upright. Garrett.

"How the hell did you get in here?" he asked, holding the thrown towel to his crotch.

"The same way I get in everything and everyone. Charm."

Simon squinted and saw he was holding a bunch of towels. So the maid let him in, then. "What time is it?"

"Time for you to tell me the plan," Mal said, plugging in the coffeemaker.

"What plan?"

He turned around. "You haven't checked your email since...? Huh. He told me you were focused, efficient. I guess you better boot up. Fuck...where is the sodding on switch for this fucking...okay, got it."

Dread washed over Simon as he realized that he hadn't actually checked his encrypted email since yesterday afternoon.

He'd been trained to check it every three hours when not in the field on an op. And it hadn't once crossed his mind to even look at his computer since Mal walked off with the minister. His focus had been Sadie and nothing else. Shit.

He strode to the safe and got his PC out, booted it up, and while waiting for his ID card to be authenticated, he slipped into jeans, for which he earned a thankful look from Mal. It also occurred to him that his boss at Fort Bragg could easily see when he last logged in.

Shit.

"You want to fill me in while I'm waiting for this?" He nodded to his PC.

"Nope. I'm the temp, remember? You may take something totally different away from your email. If I'm running the op, too right I'll tell you about it. You're running it? It's on you to figure out the nuance in that email."

Nuance. Who would have thought that word would come out of his mouth? He was a surprise. Hadn't heard anyone external to CAG draw op lines in the sand like that so succinctly since...when? Fuck. Enduring Freedom. Nearly ten years. "Well, make yourself useful with the coffee, then," he grumbled.

"What do you think I'm doing, asking it out for dinner? Jesus. It's coming." Mal shook his head and sat on the arm of the chair nearest the percolator. "I suppose it didn't occur to you to preorder breakfast and proper coffee to the room, did it?"

He was in to his computer. "Nope." Five emails. Eh, three of them were regarding admin, two of them from Barnum. "What the...?" He looked at Garrett, who stared impassively back at him.

Simon reread the email and then clicked into the second email. He looked at the ceiling for inspiration. "Are you kidding me?" he murmured.

"Here." Garrett passed him a white china mug of coffee and sat again.

"We have to prepare to save the minister ourselves if it looks like anyone else is trying to extract him? That's..."

"The dog's bollocks? I know. It's brilliant. If the Russians are sending out rumors that the CIA is going to kidnap him, imagine their surprise when we *save* him! No one expects the Spanish Inquisition," Garrett said, looking schoolkid excited for the first time.

"Seriously? Am I expected to understand what you're talking about?"

Garrett leaned forward and etched a look of fake concern on his face. "You do know I'm speaking English, right?" He spoke really slowly, sounding out every word until Simon seriously contemplated reaching down his throat to rip his larynx out.

"What did you and the minister talk about last night?" Simon asked, wondering if anything he said might give them an in, or at least a weakness to exploit.

"Women mainly. He thinks Francois is a complete dog when it comes to women, so he delights in detailing all the nitty-gritty of his exploits. He had three of his regular—well, he calls them mistresses, and who am I to judge—flown to Athens for the three weeks he's here and has them all staying at different hotels. He tells his wife he's going to a meeting, and voilà. I guess you have to give him props for his balls."

"I've followed him to...wait—let me check." Simon got his GPS watch from the nightstand and clicked through the locations he'd checked. "Four—I have him going to four hotels."

They looked at each other for a second with mirroring frowns. "Could be nothing? Just another girl he's met?" Garrett said slowly.

"Could be some other kind of meeting," Simon said with a shrug.

"Could be..." Garrett agreed softly.

* * *

Sadie got to work bright and early, feeling a little better than she had the previous morning. She'd gotten up early enough to get coffee and a pastry from the bakery around the corner from the office, and she was looking forward to a refill from Sebastian's heavenly coffee machine.

She was working very hard to keep Simon out of her mind. The sex had been incredible. Better than she remembered—more...raw and hungry. Just the thought of it sent cool ripples through her stomach. Like butterflies but sexier. Sexy butterflies. *Shit. Get a grip, girl.*

Sebastian wasn't in yet, so she grabbed a coffee from his personal stash—better to apologize later than ask for permission before—and looked at the intel messages that had come in overnight. Nothing seemed unusual, and there was nothing that needed action, but she did what she was supposed to do and went through surveillance photos from her region.

She hadn't even gotten through the first set from Turkey before the phone startled her. She looked at the black phone on her desk. The light was flashing next to Devries Construction again. Her heart stuttered as she looked around. She was alone in the office. No one to lean on for support. She picked up the phone and affected a nasal voice. "Devries. Can I help you? Certainly, please hold."

It was Platon. She looked at her cell phone. Again, he hadn't even tried it, so she assumed that it was another call orchestrated by Stratigos.

"Inventory Management, Sadie speaking." She hoped he couldn't hear her heart through the phone.

"*Koukla mou*! How are you?"

She played a hunch. "I'm great, thank you. I'm alone in the office today, so I don't have my boss breathing down my neck." She cast her eyes at the chief's empty office.

"Can you slip out for a few minutes? Stratigos wants to talk to you."

"Um...okay. Will you be there too?" Her mind started racing.

"Of course, *koukla mou*!" He named a café and a time before hanging up.

Sadie hung up the phone and breathed deeply. Was she ready for this? What was this about? Had he discovered who she was? Was he going to kill her? Test her? Invite her over for dinner? Where was Sebastian? She fumbled for her cell phone and dialed his number. It went straight to voice mail. Why hadn't she called from the office phone? She was losing her shit over one phone call. She could do this. This is what she'd been trained for. She took a breath and deleted the number from her phone and tapped her fingers on the desk as her eyes caught sight of her group photo from The Farm. There were six of them in the photo, muddy, having just completed the final physical test. All their faces were blurred out except hers. Everyone was given the same photo with only their face showing. It was a joke, but she'd loved it and brought it with her.

She took another breath and remembered her extensive training. *Use your brain to get out of trouble, not a weapon. As soon as you use a weapon, your cover will be blown.* She opened her drawer and grabbed the piece of paper that she'd used to plot out how she thought inventory management would work at the fictitious Devries Construction. She'd memorized it when she'd arrived in Athens but thought a refresher would calm her down.

Suddenly she wished she had Simon following her. Covering her back. Protecting her. *Dammit.* No she didn't. She could handle this.

* * *

At the appointed time, she arrived at the café, swinging her purse as if she had zero cares in the world. She gave them both a wide smile when she saw Platon and Stratigos sitting at a table slightly isolated from the other coffee-drinking tourists.

Platon jumped up and kissed her chastely on both cheeks. Stratigos's expression was appraising. She ordered another coffee and wondered just how jumped up on caffeine she was going to be by the end of the day.

Stratigos started. "I understand that your company constructed the new annex on the US embassy here in the city, correct?"

"Yes. I think so. It happened before I was hired, but there is a large photo of the embassy in one of the restrooms in the office." What was he angling for?

Stratigos laughed, and Platon joined in, although she could tell by his expression that he wasn't entirely sure why he was laughing.

"Appropriate positioning for the embassy, perhaps?" He guffawed again.

Sadie ignored the instinct to punch him in the face and giggled too.

"So, I would like to pay you for a copy of the construction blueprints. Say, one thousand euros for a large copy?" He held his hands out to indicate the size.

She knew exactly what was happening, and she couldn't control her glee. He was trying to recruit her with the oldest trick in the book. The one that she'd been taught to use. They were going to pay her for information anyone could easily obtain—the blueprints for all government buildings were kept in the central library—and after she took money from them once, she would belong to them. They would ask her for slightly more difficult things to find before they'd ask her for the one thing they really needed all along. When she refused, they'd show photos of her accepting money from them and tell her she was already a traitor who would go to prison.

She couldn't believe Stratigos was using it on her. And that Platon was letting him. Bastard.

"You look happy, yes? You need the money?" Stratigos asked, patting her hand.

"I can always use extra money." She smiled. "When do you need the blueprints?"

"I give you the money now, and you give me the blueprints tomorrow, yes?"

"Wow. Absolutely. I saw these shoes that I really..." She stopped herself as if she were embarrassed, but he smiled.

He passed her a small envelope, and she put it in her bag. She was absolutely sure that someone was close by taking her photo, so she ducked her head slightly. No sense in putting her face on record if she didn't have to.

The older man got up. "Excellent. You can arrange the drop-off with Platon. I have some people who are here to see me." He nodded to three men who were ostensibly looking at the menu at the entrance to the café.

She got up and shook his hand before leaving with Platon.

"I'll walk you back to your office," he said excitedly.

"Thank you," she said, tucking her arm in his. He seemed fidgety, on edge. As if he were on drugs. He laughed at nothing and wrapped his arm around her supertight.

They walked down a small back road, away from the tourists, and into the cool of the shadows. Suddenly he stopped. When she looked up at him, he crushed her mouth with his, pushing her into the opening of an alleyway. Shit.

She tore her mouth away. "Wow, Platon. What's gotten into you?" She rubbed the side of her mouth to show him that he'd hurt her, but his blazing eyes barely seemed to register her words. He pushed her against the wall, banging her head as he did.

"I need you, *koukla mou*. I've waited so long." He nuzzled her neck as his hand snaked down to her skirt.

She was about to stop him, insist he make a date to see her in the normal manner, when his hand started an upward trajectory. She slapped his hand away playfully, but before he could react, he was yanked off her.

A man in a hoodie threw him to the ground, sat on him, and punched him twice. Platon was already unconscious when the man brought his hand up for another swing. She kicked the man in the armpit to inflict the maximum amount of pain. He jumped up with a grunt, and his hood fell down.

"Simon. What are you...?" She looked down at Platon, who was stirring. Or at least moaning. "What the hell are you doing?" she hissed.

"What do you mean, what am I doing? He was attacking you. I stopped him. You expected me to walk on by?" His voice suggested he was barely containing his rage. "I should kill him." He took a step toward Platon.

"Don't move another inch," she bit out. "I *let* him touch me. He was under control. Get away from here. Get away from *me*."

He stalked off to the end of the alleyway, took one furious look back at Platon, and disappeared around the corner.

Shit, shit, shit on a stick. She thought quickly. "Platon. Are you okay? Come on—let's get you some help." She put her arm under his shoulders and levered him into a sitting position.

"What happened?" he moaned in Greek.

"We were mugged," she answered in English.

He groaned and put his damaged face in his hands.

While he got himself together, she took from her wallet a photo of people she didn't know, but who she'd told Platon were her parents, and dropped it in the alley behind him. She also grabbed a few euro coins and a fancy lipstick and casually dropped them as she bent down to help him up.

"Shall I take you to the hospital?" she asked, praying the answer would be no.

"Take me to Stratigos," he mumbled from behind a potentially broken jaw.

"Okay; lean on me," she said calmly as she walked him out of the passageway. She ducked her head, knowing that passersby would be looking at him and not wanting anyone to be able to describe her face. As she walked past a trash can, she quickly dropped the envelope of cash in it.

She hesitated at the entrance to the café. A waiter approached and she just nodded toward Stratigos, who was still talking to the three men. He went to the table and bent over to whisper in Stratigos's ear. He looked up with astonishment when he saw them, and beckoned her.

"What happened?" he asked as she deposited Platon carefully in a chair.

"We were mugged. In an alleyway down Pascis Street. It was...horrible." She made tears well up. "He just jumped out of nowhere."

Stratigos nodded to the three men, who got up and left. Then he called to the waiter. Two glasses of ouzo appeared. "Drink. It will calm your nerves," he said. "Did they take the money I gave you?"

"Yes!" she cried between fairly reasonable sobs. I think I lost a photo of my parents too." She put her hands over her face and shook as if she were crying. After a couple of minutes, she sniffed, straightened, and took some sips of the liquor in front of her.

"Here you are, my dear. Don't cry." He slipped a roll of money secured with a rubber band to her. "Keep this one safe. Go back to work; don't you worry about Platon. He will receive the best care. I promise."

She scraped her chair back. "Thank you. Please tell him to call me when he feels better."

Stratigos nodded. "I will call you tomorrow morning to arrange for you to drop off the plans."

"Okay." She sniffed and left the café, passing the three men as they returned to Stratigos's table. She looked back once, in time to see one of the guys showing Stratigos something on his phone. She hoped it was the "crime scene" that she'd planted. She'd go back and at least try to recover the money, just to cover her bases. The envelope of cash at least had his fingerprints on it, and maybe other people's too.

She worked her way back to the alleyway, eluding any surveillance, real or imaginary. It was empty. The photo, euro coins, and lipstick had disappeared. A short walk confirmed that Stratigos's money was also gone. *Dammit.*

She elected to run home to change, since she had Platon's blood on her top. It wasn't like she really worked nine to five at the construction company, although sometimes she had to remind herself of it. She'd found herself on numerous occasions rushing back to the office, like they actually cared that their fake inventory manager was late back from lunch. Most of the officers didn't go to the office for days at a time.

As soon as she got home, she changed into a clean blouse and tried to tame the stray strands that had come loose from her flower-shaped hair clips.

As she looked at herself in the mirror, she heard fast stomping steps coming from the stairwell. Her front door burst open. She flinched and flattened herself against the wall so the intruder couldn't see her.

"Where the hell are you?" a familiar voice asked.

Simon.

She un-plastered herself from the wall and stepped calmly into the main room. "What the hell are *you* doing, letting yourself into my apartment again? Didn't we cover this before?"

CHAPTER TWELVE

She stood with her hands balled on her hips, fire flashing from her eyes in what would be a fairly frightening way if he didn't still have pictures of her seminaked and against a wall in his brain.

Well, she was up to her neck in something bad, and he wasn't going to let it continue. He held up a plastic baggie. In it were a photo, some euros, and her lipstick that he was sure she'd planted, and an envelope of cash he'd actually found in the trash can near the alley. "Cover-up one oh one."

"Cover-up...what? What are you talking about?"

He wanted to say that it was a classic trained move, to leave corroborating evidence in case someone ever returned to check a story. He looked at her meaningfully, hoping she'd just admit it. She was a spy of some sort. Trained. For the US, or maybe even the enemy. God only knew what had gone on in the past year. But he was sure of this.

Semisure.

Okay, he had a feeling.

She grabbed the bag from him and peered through the plastic. "You found my money. Thank you for that. The rest..." She shrugged, tipping it out on the bed. "Well, obviously the euros are mine—I mean, no one else has euro coins." She rolled her eyes at him. "The picture is of...Who are these people, Simon? I've never seen them before in my life." She flipped over the photo to read the back and gave him a pitying look. "Mom and Dad? Really? You've met my parents, who definitely aren't these people in the photo, and you automatically think it's mine?" She flicked the photo onto the bed. "I'll give you that some things have changed since you left me. But my parents haven't."

He had never wanted to punch a wall so much in his life. Ever. He was sure...

"What about the lipstick?" he said.

She picked it up and yanked the lid off. She winced as she looked at it. "Shit, Simon. You think I'd wear that color?"

He grabbed it and looked inside. She had a point. It was dark to the point of black. He'd examined it for a microphone or a compartment that could hide a tracker but hadn't registered that the color really wasn't Sadie's style.

"What about the money?" he asked tightly.

"I'd been saving cash to buy shoes at the Attica department store. They give a discount for cash every first Friday of the month." Her voice dropped to a concerned pitch. "Are you okay, Simon? You seem really stressed. Can you talk about it?"

Fuck. Fuck. How could he have gotten this so wrong? How

was he so quick to suspect Sadie, of all people, was some kind of spy? Shit. What an idiot.

He shook his head and turned away from her, taking in the view from her window—that of a dirty alley and some Dumpsters. He saw some stacked folders on her desk with a construction company's branding all over them. Was he really so off the mark?

"Come here, Simon. What's really wrong?"

He tried again. "The man you had coffee with today—he's a very well-documented anarchist. He's been in and out of jail for the majority of the past forty years. He was responsible for a knife attack on the Greek finance minister, the car bomb that blew up a member of their parliament—with his two children—and at least five other firebombings. He's dangerous, and I don't want you to see him again." He watched her expression carefully for a tell, any kind of sign that he wasn't going crazy.

Her eyes narrowed. "Really? How fascinating. Platon's uncle? Wow. I had no idea he had such interesting relatives."

This *wasn't* the reaction he was hoping for. He sat on a stool by some kind of dresser and put his head in his hands. "Why are you here, Sadie? I can't move in this town without bumping into you. You're distracting me so much that I'm seeing shadows where there are none. I just don't know what to do." Maybe pity would work. He stuck his thumbnails into the corners of his eyes before raising his face and rubbing them. He knew they would be red, and he wondered if she'd think he was close to tears. Then he wondered if he wanted her to think he'd ever be close to tears. *Fuck. Fuck.*

He held a hand out to her and she took it, concern etched across her face. He pulled her gently onto his knee and wrapped his arms around her, squeezing her as if he were using her life force.

Her hand started stroking his back, soothing and slow.

He very slowly placed his face at her neck, inhaling her familiar scent, took a deep breath, and made it shudder a bit.

She held him tighter, shifting against his leg. Well, maybe she thought it was his leg. He closed his eyes. When he wasn't looking at her, lying to her, trying to get information from her...in that moment in time, he was in love with her again, as if nothing else mattered. Nothing else affected them.

He wasn't hiding anything from her or watching her hide things from him. With his eyes closed, they were engaged again. Maybe on their honeymoon. He wanted his Sadie.

He pulled away from her and clasped her face in his hands, forcing himself to look at her. The concern in her eyes had gone, leaving something anticipatory. He was sure it matched a look in his eyes. But he closed his again. Only then could he be honest with the woman in his arms.

He moved his mouth to hers, barely touching it, allowing their breath to mingle. Sharing that thing that kept them alive. Her tongue touched his lower lip so lightly he wondered if he'd imagined it. But then he felt its touch again, and he captured her tongue in his mouth. Still gently, still quietly.

They kissed as if they were kissing for the first time. Insistent but giving. He tasted every part of her mouth, felt the swirl of her tongue against his. Just that made his stomach tighten with the knowledge that something special was happening be-tween them.

Sadie's eyes were closed as he kissed her chin and neck. He lifted her as he stood, her eyes opening as he put her down. He avoided them. He watched his fingers smooth the dark blond hair from her face and then watched her fingers as she slowly unfastened the buttons on his shirt. She pulled the tails from his waistband and, running her hands over his chest, swiped the shirt off his shoulders. As he did the same with hers, she unzipped her skirt and let it drop to the floor.

His hands reached for her as if they had a mind of their own. No will he'd ever possessed could have kept them at his sides. He stroked her neck, down to her shoulders, and then lightly ran his hands over the swell of her breasts. Her eyes closed as he did.

He continued down her soft stomach, and his fingers just lightly floated over the front of her panties, making her suck in her breath and close her eyes.

His dick was straining against his pants, and for a second he enjoyed the sensation of the pressure building in him. The tightness of his muscles and the hardness of his arousal. His hands returned to her shoulders as she brought him against her.

He ground his dick against her as her hips pressed back. "You make me crazy for you, Sadie. This is what happens whenever I think about you."

Her hand wriggled between them as she found her mark. She stroked him through his pants for a second and then un-did them, pushing them carefully to the floor. She stepped back from him for a second with an impenetrable look on her face.

* * *

"This is just us here, okay?" she said. "Nothing else...outside this door." She glanced at the entrance to her apartment. "Not our past—just us, here alone." She was lying about the past part. She wanted their past so badly. Wanted to feel loved by him. She knew it was an illusion, maybe even a delusion—after all, a few minutes ago he'd been accusing her of being exactly what she was. But he seemed tortured, sad, and stressed in a way she'd never seen before.

He closed his eyes and swallowed. "Of course. I...understand."

"Open your eyes," she commanded.

He did. She unhooked her bra from the front and slipped out of her panties. His eyes darkened as they roamed over her body, but he didn't step toward her. What was he fighting? His dick wasn't fighting anything. It seemed to be reaching out to her.

She smiled, but instead of walking to him, she eased herself onto the bed and then lay there, head propped on one hand as she playfully patted the cover. She wanted to feel free of the lies and the anger she'd been holding on to for so long.

In a flash he was on her, pressing every part of himself over her. He wrapped his arms tightly around her neck and shoulders and kissed her with a fever. She felt as if she were being absorbed into him, as if every part of her were wrapped up in him. Her heart was as turned on as the rest of her.

"I need you," she whispered against his mouth.

"You'll have me, sweetheart. I just want to have you first." He braced himself on his arms and lowered his head to her breasts. They seemed to swell and reach to him as just his breath on them made her nipples hard. He sucked and bit gently, pulling away to blow cool air on the wet tips, making her wriggle on the bed. Her legs dropped open, and she hooked her ankles around his calves, trying to urge him into her. She was filled with heat that could only be sated with him inside her.

He easily dislodged her ankles as he moved down her body. She was torn. She wanted him to fill her up, to feel his weight on her as he made love to her, but she remembered what this felt like.

The unusual breeze from the window billowed the sheer curtains, and light made patterns on them. It made her feel like she was in a movie, that she wasn't real. That this wasn't real. She was fine with that. It didn't feel real. It was too good to be real.

She was so wet. Had been since she sat on his lap and felt his dick against her. He'd never wanted her like this before. Not with the immediate reaction that his body gave. And she'd never reacted this way to him either.

He blew against her, making her jump and open her legs wider for him. He laughed at her obvious acquiescence, or brazenness, but she didn't care.

He knelt between her legs and held them open until his own legs were bracing them. And then he dipped his head.

The tip of his tongue brushed against her clitoris, lightly, as if gauging her reaction. Her body jerked. He did it again and she moaned. *More. I need more.*

Her hands gripped the bed covers in anticipation of his next touch. He used his shoulders this time to move her legs, exposing more of her to him. She tipped her hips, looking for his lips or tongue.

A strong tongue lick made her jump. It traveled from her ass, slowly to her clit, circled it a couple of times and then back. Pushing for entry again at her ass. Fingers probed everywhere. His tongue flicked at her clit and then laved it. Then flicked at it again while his fingers, seemingly all of them, explored every entrance and every part of her. Her mind felt as if it were melting inside her, rendering any reasonable thought impossible. Heat flooded her lower back, taking her to the edge of the wave that was uniquely Simon's. His fingers stroked inside her as his tongue pushed her, further and further, until she came, crashing and pulsing around his fingers.

He withdrew his fingers and licked where they had been, soothing the knife-edge of her climax. "I owed you that for last night," he said, sliding back up her body with a wry smile on his face.

She grinned. "No you didn't. Sixty euros maybe, but..."

He smothered her words with a kiss as he slid right inside her. She gasped as she felt him completely filling her in one stroke. She tipped her hips up and wrapped her legs around him, wanting to feel everything, the muscles in his butt flexing as he pushed into her again and again, the sweat making his back cool in the breeze, and the tightness of his thighs. For a second she wished she had a mirror above her bed instead of a fan, but that thought was driven from her as he picked up his pace. He thrust into her faster and faster, groaning her name, as if he wanted to hear the sound of it. She reveled in the need she felt in him, the surrender to her body. She felt powerful and wanted as he clasped one arm around her, holding her to his chest as he heaved out two more breaths and came, shuddering inside her. "Sadie," he breathed as he rested his head on her breasts.

She left her legs wrapped around him. She felt loved. Even if she wasn't. She felt loved, and she hadn't felt that way in over a year. She wanted him to feel it too. She stroked his back and rubbed her cheek lightly against the top of his head until his breath evened out and his muscles relaxed around her.

Safe. Protected. Honest. If only for a few hours.

She closed her eyes.

CHAPTER THIRTEEN

I'm having a bit of a problem." Simon's voice rumbled through her dreamless sleep and roused her.

She started when she realized that they had both slept in exactly the same position as they'd finished having sex in. Exactly the same. "What's the problem?" she teased, knowing precisely what his problem was.

"I'm...stiff?" he offered.

She laughed and squeezed her muscles around a fast-hardening dick.

"Jesus, thank God you're awake. I woke up like this, and I didn't feel like I could move in case..." He groaned as she shifted her hips.

"In case it felt like you were humping an unconscious woman?"

"I wasn't going to put it exactly like that, but that's the gist of it, yes."

"Thank God I *am* awake, then," she said, wriggling beneath him and stroking the bottoms of her feet along his legs.

"Come here." In one move he was kneeling between her legs and hauling her up onto his lap without breaking contact.

She half gasped at the depth of him within her and half laughed at how smoothly he'd done it. She centered her body around him and sat up, bracing her hands on his knees, leaning back a little.

He gripped her hips and pushed her down harder as he thrust upward. He moved her hands down to the bed and watched himself slide inside her. His eyes were so intense that she wondered if he was going to come at just the sight of where they were joined. But he looked back up at her and licked his thumb. He splayed his hand over her stomach, slipping his wet thumb onto her clit.

She jumped and tightened at the touch. Even her nipples hardened. He stroked her with every thrust.

Sadie found her place, the rush of feeling that was his, the tightening and fizzing of everything inside her as she came, gasping. He stopped to watch her as she did, naked desire or need on his face.

And then, as her breathing normalized, his expression changed. He was lost somewhere. He wasn't moving. She wanted him back.

She took his hand from between her legs and licked his thumb. His eyes flickered back to life as his gaze found hers. Then she slipped his forefinger into her mouth and sucked on it. Licked it with the tip of her tongue and then drew it all the way in. He watched avidly as he started moving inside her again. Then his eyes closed as his hands resumed pulling her hips down onto him. He thrust again and again and then threw his head back as he came, all his muscles tensing, making the most beautiful picture for her to hold in her memory.

He held her for a moment and then lifted her off him. He winced as he straightened his legs.

She laughed, hoping to retain some of the lightheartedness they'd had before. "You feeling your age, old man?"

He stretched, face half on the pillow. "You have no idea." His words faded into a groan that was pain- rather than pleasure induced.

She was scared for him to go. Suddenly scared for what that meant. She was lying to him. Her very presence here was a lie. There was nothing, except her body, that wasn't a lie. As soon as he walked out of her door, they would be back to where they'd been this morning.

She let him rest there for a minute and then reached for her bedside table. She opened the drawer and took out some Greek massage oil. Having Simon in her bed felt normal, back when her life was normal. When he'd been on missions, he'd often come back with aches and pains and sore muscles. She'd always tried to welcome him home with a massage.

She climbed on top of him and poured oil between her hands. Softly she smoothed it down his back until she reached his butt cheeks. Then she dug in and massaged every muscle that used to hurt him. Every place that he used to try to stretch out when he thought she wasn't looking.

He grunted into his pillow, and the sound made her smile. She worked on his back for a while, letting her mind wander to some happier moments they'd spent together. Including the hours just spent behind closed doors, leaving the rest of the world outside.

No past, no jobs—nothing except them. She'd even managed to let go of her anger about how he'd picked her up.

She continued to massage, knowing that as soon as she stopped, there wouldn't be more sex like there used to be, but they would have to get up and he'd have to leave.

She knew she'd have to sanitize her apartment now that he had suspicions about her. Not one thing could remain in her apartment that would suggest that she worked for the CIA. She had no doubt that when he'd had time to think about it some more, he'd remember the thousand euros he'd given back to her and for which buying shoes wasn't really a good enough excuse. He'd return and go through her apartment methodically until he found something incriminating.

Half of her wished that she could tell him. Just even for the courtesy that they were in the same city and working for the same side. But that again was a big hesitation. Why was he here, and why hadn't his chain of command alerted their office that they had operatives here?

She looked at the clock. *Shit.* It was nearly three. She slapped his butt. "Come on, old man. I've played hooky long enough. I'll be lucky to still have a job when I get back."

He rolled over. "I need a shower," he said, sitting up and nodding toward the bathroom.

She picked up his pants and threw them at him. "You can shower at your place, mister." She thought fast. "I get about thirty centiliters of hot water with decent pressure. You are not taking that away from me." She smiled and wrapped a robe around herself as he put on his clothes. "Here." She handed a small bottle of water to him as he was slipping on his shoes. "Don't dehydrate."

"Yes, ma'am," he said as he opened the front door. His voice was serious. "Don't leave town or anything."

She bristled. The door was open; the vacuum of forgetfulness was punctured. "If you had any right to tell me what to do, I'd remind you that I live here. I have a job here. I'm not going anywhere. Now get!" She tried to smile, but it didn't reach her eyes—hell, she could tell it barely reached her mouth.

The door shut behind him, and she got moving. She smoothed down the comforter and put a big laptop bag on it. She slid her secure PC in it and took the magazine out of the handgun her brother had left her. She wrapped both pieces in a towel and slid them into the bag.

Then she hesitated. She'd been pretty clean when she'd taken this apartment. She deliberately kept it to one room that doubled as a bedroom and living area, a kitchen and a bathroom. The smaller the living area, the fewer places to forget things in situations like the one she was in now, and the easier it would be to pack up necessities if her cover was blown, or worse.

And that reminded her. She had a go bag. Something she could grab and run with. Passports, cash in multiple currencies, chargers for virtually any electrical device, some burner phones, some travel toiletries, and some hats, scarves, scissors, and two colors of hair dye. If Simon found it, he would know for sure. Shit. That meant she wouldn't have anything here for emergencies.

Damn that man. She couldn't walk to work with a laptop bag and a backpack—it would either confirm his suspicions, should he be watching her, or make him think that she was, in fact, leaving town. She redistributed it all in her laptop bag and her purse, and sighed. It made her feel a little less safe at home without her emergency kit there.

After a quick shower and a change of clothes, she headed out for the office to dump the stuff. She could sense him, or someone, following her as soon as she left her apartment building. Whoever it was, they were good. She snaked around the streets without a care in the world, walking fast, ambling and window shopping, trying to get a bead on her surveillant's face. She couldn't; he was very careful. Pretty much all she could ascertain was that he was actually male and that it wasn't Simon.

So he wasn't alone here. His team must be here too, and despite how they had just spent the afternoon, he still suspected her of something. She'd considered for a moment that Stratigos's men might be following her, but she didn't think they would be that skilled. The man following her definitely had stellar tradecraft.

Ambling to a corner and then, as soon as she was out of sight, running around the next one gave her time to hit the alleyway behind her office and sneak in the back way before her tail could catch up. There were throngs of tourists around, so at least he would think that he'd just lost her and not that she herself was using *her* tradecraft.

She ran up the back stairs to her office, dumped her bags at her desk, and slumped into her chair, panting. Safe.

But she really needed to work out more.

* * *

When Garrett returned to the hotel, he looked pissed and hot. Things that inexplicably made Simon happy. "What did you discover?" he asked as Garrett threw himself into the other armchair.

"Are you sure this isn't some wild-goose chase, mate? I mean, she's just a girl who's chosen the wrong guy to get involved with. She might be useful as an asset if you actually find out that old anarchist bastard is up to something, but apart from that..." He looked at Simon expectantly.

Could Simon have been wrong about her? That afternoon he'd forgotten everything that had been coursing through his mind all week, distracted by a Sadie he barely recognized. He put his elbows on his knees and rubbed his hands over his face.

"Oh Jesus, not you too. The last Yank I was here with got his knickers in a wad over some girl too. Does your military training come with a course at the romance school? You can't mix work and women." He paused, shaking his head and looking out of the window. "Okay, tell me about it. Don't leave out any details. Especially the naked details." He leaned forward, virtually rubbing his hands together.

It was only fair to be honest with him, since they were working together. "She's my ex-fiancée. We broke up last year, and I haven't seen her since. Until here. She quit her job and moved here, it seems." He shrugged.

"Most women just cut their hair," Garrett said.

"She did that too." Simon sank back in the chair and looked at the ceiling. "I could have sworn she was doing something she shouldn't be. Hanging out with people she shouldn't. And I beat up her boyfriend this morning, and when I returned to the scene of the crime, there was stuff left there, like evidence that had nothing to do with me."

"Hold it, hold it. You beat up her boyfriend this morning,

and this afternoon you had me follow her? I'm not fucking here to help you with your domestic problems. I sweated my arse off waiting for her to leave her apartment. You know it's over a hundred fucking degrees outside, don't you? Jesus." He shook his head. "This *is* a circus Barnum is running here. You know I'm putting this afternoon's duties in my report, right?"

Simon couldn't even be bothered to object. "Sure, whatever. I had a good reason to suspect..."

Garrett leaned in. "I think you're doing one of two things. You're either subconsciously looking for a reason to keep close to her or finding a reason to keep away from her. When you figure it out, we'll all be happier. So figure it out."

Simon got up and looked out of the window at the masses of people in front of the Greek parliament building.

"So what's the plan for saving Stamov? Do we have any of the necessary equipment?" Garrett asked.

Goddamn him. Simon hadn't even put more than a cursory thought into Barnum's instructions to develop a plan to lift the finance minister.

"I don't have one yet, at least not one that holds water. There are just too many variables. If there are ten men trying to kidnap him, one of us on watch isn't going to be able to do much. It's a logistics issue more than anything else."

"I can get weapons. I mean, I have weapons. But I can get pretty much anything we might need as far as hardware goes. And last summer I shagged a lovely Greek lady cop. She could be useful. Her dad's fairly high up, so she gets pretty much anything she wants. It's how things work here."

"Are you sure she's still talking to you? I mean, have you spoken to her since you 'shagged' her?" Simon couldn't honestly believe anyone still talked to Garrett voluntarily.

"I don't need to. She knew what we were about. I'm always clear—no entanglements and no phone numbers. Except I had hers before we...well, you know what I mean." He looked at his phone. "Yup." He flashed the screen to Simon. All he saw was a blur of flesh and some very red lips. "I've still got it."

"Was that a naked photo of her?"

"Yeah." Garrett smiled, seemingly lost in a memory. Then he looked up at Simon. "It's not what you think. She insisted I take it to remember her by."

He didn't want to give Garrett an inch, but that kind of cop sounded exactly like the kind of rule-breaking person they could use on side. "Why don't you make contact with her? Just in case."

Garrett frowned. "That's not how you do it. You don't give them advance notice so they have time to remember that they hate you. You have to spring your presence on them, overwhelm them. Bloody hell, it's no wonder you've been having issues with your long-lost beloved."

Simon wanted to punch the shit-eating grin off Garrett's face, but instead he threw a sofa cushion at him. "I'm just amazed you're still alive, especially if you go around hitting and quitting."

"One of my many fine talents." He shrugged. "So do you want me to put my sources on notice?"

"Sure, I guess so. I have zero idea what we'd need, though. We're going to have to figure out exactly where he could be snatched from and how."

"How the hell are we supposed to do that?" Garrett said.

"We just plan it like we were kidnapping him ourselves."

CHAPTER FOURTEEN

Shit on a stick!"

"Did you break a nail, darling?" Sebastian's droll voice came from the kitchen.

"Um, have you checked the intel telexes this morning?" They called them telexes still, even though they no longer came rattling into the office on a teleprinter.

"Not before my coffee, darling; it's bad for my heartburn," he replied, emerging with two tiny cups of coffee. Under normal circumstances, she'd squee with delight at being offered one without having to beg or bargain.

"You better get your Tums, then, because you're not going to like it."

It had been three days since Sadie had seen Simon. Stratigos hadn't called about the plans that she had waiting on her desk, and the office Christmas party fund was now two thousand euros in the black. She'd just started to relax, to go about her work as normal.

Sebastian sat at his desk, input his password, and scrolled down. "Ah, shit on a stick," he said quietly.

Numerous sources had written from all over the region saying that they were hearing that some known suppliers were being put on notice for a large purchase out of Athens. And although no one specified the actual requests, the suppliers were known for the procurement of anything from switchblades to enriched uranium. Nothing about this was comforting.

"This is really bad news. Really bad," Sebastian said. "We're going to have to call the director back from his golf vacation in the Costa del Sol. He is not going to be a happy bunny. Not one bit."

Sadie felt a little out of her depth. She hadn't been here long enough to cultivate any deep assets in the city. None except Platon. She cursed her single-mindedness about him. No doubt he was into something, but he wouldn't have good enough connections to put so many high-level suppliers on alert. She'd been wasting her time with him.

"Tell me what to do. I'll do anything...even pick up your dry cleaning." Why had she said that?

"I know you want to help, but I don't think my having a clean jacket is going to stop world terrorism."

She went to the whiteboard that usually held lunch orders when the office was full. She wrote the number seventeen in big numbers with a circle around it.

"What's that?" Sebastian asked.

"The number of days until Air Force One is wheels down in Athens." She put the cap firmly back on the marker and replaced it in the tray with a thud.

"So you're in charge of office morale?"

"Just keeping us focused. Now tell me. What do you need me to do?"

"Call the director and touch base with our station in Istanbul and Paris. Ask who their sources for this intel are and how reliable they've been in the past. See what kind of commitment you get from them to delve deeper for you." His eyes flickered to the clock. "I want a full sitrep at midday. Questions?"

She'd never seen him so alive and decisive. She guessed that's why he was on the senior officer pay grade. "None. I'm on it."

She'd just pulled up the contact details of the city offices, when the desk phone rang. Sebastian looked at the light flashing and glared at her.

It was the Devries Construction line. She swiveled her chair away from Sebastian's disapproval and answered it in her nasal receptionist's voice.

It was Stratigos this time, and for a second she wondered if Platon was still too injured to talk. They'd texted a couple of times, but that's all she'd heard from him. When she put him through, he wasted no time with small talk. "I need those plans."

She fingered the plans that were still on her desk. "I have them here, sir," she said, hoping he'd like the deference.

"Please come to the café where we met before. Ten minutes?"

There was absolutely no time that day, or even the next, that she'd be able to slip away. "I'm afraid I'm really bus—"

But he'd already hung up. *Shit sticks.* Sadie turned to Sebastian, who still had his stern face on. "I have to slip out for a few minutes. I'll be right back—I promise."

He shook his head silently, then turned his attention back to his PC.

She hesitated for a second before she grabbed her purse and the plans and ran for the stairs. She clocked the time at ten thirty. She would be back by eleven or die trying.

She arrived at the café to find Stratigos and Platon waiting for her, with the three men she'd seen there before sitting around the table behind them.

She took the open chair, placed the rolled-up plans on the table, and looked at Platon. "How are you feeling, sweetie?" She smiled and put her hand on his arm, but he didn't meet her eyes.

Stratigos took the plans and leaned forward. "Platon tells me that you weren't mugged. Indeed, Platon still had his wallet on him when you brought him back to me."

Sadie's blood ran cold. She'd forgotten about his wallet. But she smiled. This was why they paid her the big bucks. Or at least this would be why they paid her the big bucks, if they ever paid anyone big bucks. "Aw, Platon. I told you that you were unconscious, remember? When we were walking back?"

He met her eyes for the first time with a frown. His hand went to his head.

She leaned in and looked Stratigos in the eye. "He was unconscious for about a minute and a half, which is when the man took my things. He threw my purse on the ground. Platon had fallen on his back, so his wallet couldn't have been accessed anyway...But hold on a moment." She paused and looked at her purse and pushed her chair back a little as if she were just remembering something. "The mugger only went for my purse. He took the envelope straight out and dumped the rest. It was as if he *knew* it was in there." She looked at both Platon and Stratigos and then the three men behind them with purpose, as if she were deciding which one orchestrated the mugging. "Which one of you took the general's money?" she asked the three men.

Suddenly the dynamic changed. They all started talking at once, pleading with Stratigos in Greek, reaching hands out to him as they spoke.

"Enough," Stratigos said. "Enough." Silence fell. "You have money now, so the matter is settled." He looked at his muscle. "I will find out what happened to you, you can be sure of that."

She beamed. "Good. And when you do, I hope you punish them for what they did to Platon." She deliberately softened her voice as she said his name. Platon gave her a small smile, which was pretty much all he could do, given the cut on his lower lip.

"Thank you for the plans. Can I rely on you for"—he shrugged—"other favors?"

"Any friend of Platon's is a friend of mine," she said brightly. "But I have to go. I had to sneak out while my boss was in a meeting." She stood and slung her purse over her shoulder. "Call me, sweetie," she said to Platon and squeezed his shoulder as she went past, bussing the top of his head as she did.

As soon as she rounded the corner, she checked her watch and started to run. She'd successfully turned the tables on their accusation. Brains, not bullets, as they said at The Farm. If she could get back to work and get all the information that Sebastian needed, she would consider this a good day.

She called the Paris CIA station first, because they were already up. She knew the Istanbul office opened later because it stayed open later. Although they worked from the embassy for security, they often worked late into the evening off-site. It was easier going to work without being notable when there were hundreds of people coming and going through the embassy grounds.

She was put through to a woman called Stephanie. The directory said that she was a tech analyst, and there was no hiding that she was surprised to hear from Sadie.

"Wow. There are people out there, after all. I mean, I'd heard rumors..."

Sadie frowned at the phone. "Excuse me?"

"Sorry. They keep us in the basement here, and I've been sending out intel reports for six months and no one has ever called me about any of them. We all assumed they were being deep filed, if you know what I mean," she said. Sadie could hear her typing as she spoke and envied her ability to multitask like that.

"Not this one. I'm looking at telex number PA40045. What can you tell me about that?"

Stephanie typed for a moment before speaking again. "It was chatter picked up in a bar in the thirteenth arrondissement in the city and then corroborated by an email. It came from an unknown client asking for a hold on what the emailer termed 'lift equipment,' which we assume is code for something."

"Do you know where it came from?" Sadie asked.

"Athens. The account itself couldn't be traced. But I can tell you that it was sent using a hotel mobile server, which was his only mistake. Hotel servers aren't known for their security."

Her mind blown by this whole side of the business she knew nothing about, Sadie scribbled down some of what Stephanie said. "Wow," she said. "I need to remember your telephone number."

"It's nice to be appreciated. I'll tell the rest of the guys here. Do you want to know which hotel it came from?"

She kicked herself. How could she forget to ask? "Yes, please—that would be awesome."

"The email came from the Agropolis Hotel."

Sadie half knew she was going to say that, but it was still a shock to hear it said. It was where Platon worked. Which meant she needed to tell Sebastian about her work to date. Which again was half a relief and half-horrible. She'd desperately wanted to reel Platon and Stratigos in herself to prove to the director, and her father—and possibly even herself—that she was capable of being really good at her job.

* * *

Simon was in Sadie's apartment again. But this time, he wasn't going to tell anyone. Not even Sadie. He hoped to be gone before she got home—a ghost visit.

He planned on spending less than thirty minutes there. He just needed to be sure. Just for his peace of mind. The thought of Sadie involved in something bad turned his stomach. And he had a really strong stomach. But he was sure there was something off about his ex-fiancée.

He shut and locked her front door. And methodically made his way from the left-hand side of the door. He checked the thick doorframe to make sure there were no hidden compartments. Then he checked under the rug and behind every picture on the wall. Nothing. Bedside table—aha! He opened the drawer and found a strange shiny, black, pebble-looking thing. A microphone? A scrambler? He picked it up and flicked the switch. As it buzzed into action, and he realized what it was, he nearly dropped the thing. Juggling to catch it, he batted it back in the drawer. Shit, Sadie. A vibrator?

He tried to concentrate on the job instead of imagining exactly what Sadie did with her toy. He pulled out the drawer, feeling the sides and underneath and around the back of the nightstand. Nothing.

He looked under the bed and under the mattress—nothing. He contemplated pulling the seams open, but there was really no hiding that. So instead he felt around the seams for anything that didn't belong here.

With steady, practiced moves, he continued to make his way around the room, opening drawers and feeling for anything that shouldn't be there. Three-quarters of the way around, he suddenly realized what a shit he was being to her. He was searching his ex-fiancée's apartment. The push and pull in his brain was seriously doing a number on his head. There was something off about her: therefore, she must be a criminal or into something bad. She had a boyfriend yet had slept with Simon too—was that a concrete reason for searching her rooms? Her boyfriend's uncle—or whatever he was—was a known anarchist, or a terrorist by any other name, so obviously she had to be involved. He finished the apartment and sat down on the bed and held his head to send those doubting voices away.

He was about to get up and leave, when he caught her scent. He started for a moment, looking toward the window for an escape, but there was no sound, no footsteps on the stairs. It was coming from the bed. He lifted the pillow to his face. *Oh my God.* Just the smell of her perfume and shampoo made him want her. He buried his face into the pillow and just inhaled for a couple of moments. Blood started pulsing noticeably through his dick. Dammit. He put his hand in his lap and tried to think his way past an erection. But his body refused to listen.

There was absolutely no way he was staying there after that. Beating off in an absent girl's apartment reeked of stalker–serial killer. He had to get outside. He put the pillow back down, arranged the covers, and headed out, closing the door behind him.

As his erection subsided, he realized that she obviously couldn't be involved in what he thought she was involved in. Which was good. It meant he could just zoom in and ask her what the fuck was going on with her boyfriend. Because now he was sure. He wanted Sadie all to himself. All. To. Himself.

CHAPTER FIFTEEN

Sadie was still at work. She'd briefed Sebastian on the things Stephanie had told her—it turned out that he knew about the software they were using. It also turned out that the Athens station was getting its own Stephanie at the beginning of the following year. Nice.

Now all that had to be tied in was Platon. Possibly.

"There is one thing that may or may not be related," she began.

Sebastian put his pen down and gave her his full attention, which unnerved her. Somehow she thought she'd tell him while he was distracted by the bigger picture.

"So the guy I've been pretending to see..."

"Pretending?" Sebastian's eyes shot up into his thick salt-and-pepper hairline.

She took a deep breath. "Yes, pretending."

"You didn't sleep with him?" He crossed his arms and swung his chair around, putting his feet up on the desk. "You lied to me?"

"Only sligh—yes, I did."

"Carry on."

"Okay. The background is that when I was screening the new employees at the G20 hotel, I came across this one guy. He wrote on his application that he was a mobile-phone sales assistant, which he was. But on the application he completed for the cell phone company, he had listed a bunch of qualifications that he hadn't listed on his application to work at the hotel. He was an engineer, graduated top of his class in electronic engineering with a minor in mechanics. I wondered why he was applying for work as a security guard.

"So I just followed him. More as an exercise than anything else. You know, at The Farm they tell you—"

He interrupted. "Yes, they tell you to practice your skills by following random people and seeing how much you can find out about their lives. I know."

She nodded. "So I did that. I let him pick me up in a bar, and I've been fending off any more than kissing for about a month.

"Last week he introduced me to Stratigos—this man"—she showed him a photo—"who seems to run an anarchist cell. Very anti-American. He trapped me a few days ago. The phone call I got today? I let him pay me for the plans of the US embassy annex. I delivered them to him. He asked me if I'd be willing to do him more favors." She shrugged. "It's a textbook move."

"Where's the money?" Sebastian asked.

She smiled. "It's a long story, but I got him to pay me twice. There's two thousand euros in the safe." She nodded toward the huge, very old steel safe that took up a corner of the office.

He nodded and sighed. "Let's hope we're all still here to have a good Christmas party then."

It was a CIA tradition that any operative who was given cash would put it toward their Christmas party. They justified it to themselves because they couldn't give the money back to the criminal, and they couldn't hand it to the police or their cover would be blown. If they sent it to Langley, they'd basically be exporting illegal money. So they made the decision decades ago that they would pump it back into the local economy by having Christmas parties.

"I want lobster at the party," she said, happy that he wasn't pissed at her.

"In December? You'd be better off just drinking fifty dollars' worth of Pepto-Bismol. Anyway. Back to your story."

"Right. I don't think it could be a coincidence that Platon works at the same hotel that the email came from. Do you?" she asked.

"Do I think it could be a coincidence? Of course it could. It's one of the biggest hotels in Athens. It also might not be a coincidence. But regardless, it's not enough to go on. See if you can find out more. Preferably before the director gets back."

She nodded and went back to her computer screen. She was sure it would only be a matter of time before Stratigos called again.

She called the Istanbul office, but they said they'd just been repeating what a source had mentioned in passing. The CIA operative hadn't wanted to ask more about it because he was undercover and wasn't prepared to "show himself" for such a tiny bit of information. She couldn't blame him. So the only lead she had was Platon. But she wanted to do her due diligence, so she called their contact at the hotel for a list of their guests and employees who were present at the hotel the day before.

While she waited for the list, she considered emailing Simon. She still had his email address on her personal email. She'd thought about deleting it, pulling up the contact and hovering her thumb over the DELETE CONTACT button, but had always come up with a reason not to. She knew she had a million excuses, but somehow she'd convinced herself that each one was the right reason not to. But in truth, she'd been putting off deleting the contact because she'd still had hope that he might show up somewhere and sweep her off her feet. Until, of course, she'd received her training. If not for her current job, his appearing here in Athens would have been a dream come true. She'd have told him everything she'd felt and made him talk about their relationship. But she couldn't now. She had too many secrets to hide herself to start a "let's be honest" conversation.

The next time she looked up it was six p.m. Her shoulders hurt and her stomach was rumbling. She stretched and yawned.

"Hungry?" Sebastian asked, stretching the same way.

"Desperately. I'll go. If I stay sitting here, I'm going to get bedsores. Or chair sores or something."

"Here." He threw rumpled euros on the desk. "Go get us the biggest, nastiest pizza you can find. I need food." He dragged out the last word and then yawned himself.

When she got back with the greasy, amazing-smelling pizza, Sebastian had already gotten out a hidden bottle of bourbon and two glasses. Until she clapped eyes on it, she hadn't realized how badly she needed a drink.

"Lemme grab some ice," she said, already halfway to the kitchen.

"Sure, if you're okay ruining it," he grumbled.

"I am okay with that," she said with a grin.

He shook his head in slow despair. She loved it when he pretended to be exasperated with the younger generation.

They drank and ate, and she belched, making him laugh unreasonably hard. And then they drank some more, and then a good hour after they finished eating, they reheated the leftovers and started eating again.

When the last slice had disappeared, Sebastian pressed his fist to his chest and made a face. "Hello, heartburn, my old friend."

Sadie giggled, and when she started, she found it hard to stop.

"You wait. Twenty years and you'll be a card-carrying member of the Tums club." He popped a few in his mouth and chewed.

"You poor old man." She shook her head in pretend sympathy, and he just groaned.

"Do you remember your time at The Farm?" she asked him.

"Jesus, child. I'm not *that* old. Of course I do."

She giggled and hiccupped, and giggled again, trying and failing the first time to rest her chin on her hand. She was wasted. For a second she realized that she'd probably have to sleep at the office that night. She didn't reckon her chances at getting home by herself were very good...unless, of course, Simon was following her again. Simon.

"I think maybe one time, before I'd moved into operations, I think maybe someone made me their mark." She could feel her face flushing, and she didn't know if it was the alcohol or the fact that she was confessing to a weakness.

"Really? How so?" he asked, propping his own chin on both hands, with his elbows resting on his desk, looking for all the world like an eager schoolgirl.

She giggled again. And then searched her pickled brain for the thoughts to try to articulate. "I was in Mumbai in 2011—no wait, 2012."

"Oh. Right. You were there for the bombing?" He dropped his hands and looked sincerely interested.

"I was hurt in the shock of the blast. Not seriously. But this man who'd been smiling at me on the plane 'just happened'"—she used her fingers in slightly uncoordinated air quotes—"to pick me up and take me back to my hotel. But I hadn't told him the name of my hotel. And he got me a bit drunk and took me to my room, although I hadn't told him the room number. And then he slept with me, fully clothed, until the morning. And then he asked if he could see me again."

Sebastian sat up straight and frowned. "Classic. Wow. Nicely done, whoever it was." He smiled.

"I almost married him," she said, and watched as his face fell.

"Jesus Christ, Sadie. Who was he? Did you ever find out? I don't remember reading about this in your file." He shoved his glasses on. "That's a serious breach..."

She puffed out her cheeks. "No. He was on our side, as it turns out. Military, anyway. Secret. Which is why he's not a part of my record. But ever since my first week in the field, I wondered why he picked me—whether he was trying to get close to my father, or something worse. Was I his mission? Collateral damage on some other mission...?" She could feel herself start to well up, so she stopped talking and looked at her PC, even though it was clear that she was in no state to work.

Sebastian burst out laughing. Cackled, even. He threw his head back and guffawed, almost falling off his chair.

How could he? She looked at him in what she hoped was a disapproving look, except she couldn't be sure she'd pulled it off because her face was a little numb.

"You complete idiot." He started laughing again. "You're—so—*innocent*," he choked out.

"What are you talking about?"

"We all do that, Sadie. You take young men into a classroom and teach them how to get women to trust them, what do you *think* they're going to do with that information? Only use it for good? They're young men. Of course they're going to use their skills to get to know a beautiful woman." He started laughing again. "How do you think I persuaded Netta to go out with me? My charm and good looks?" He laughed so hard that he snorted.

Sadie half laughed, half hiccupped again. And then when she saw him crying with laughter, she couldn't help but laugh herself. Was she really that stupid? Had Simon just seen her and liked her? Was it as simple as that? Had she been holding this grudge so long that she'd convinced herself that he must have been doing something nefarious?

"Did you ever tell Netta?" she asked.

He sobered immediately. "No, of course not. She'd kill me,

and I'm not even joking. If you mention this to her..."

Sadie started laughing and held up her hands in surrender. "I won't; I promise. Your secret is safe with me. As long as you keep supplying me with your coffee." She put on an innocent smile.

He groaned. And chuckled again. "Sweet, innocent Sadie," he said. "So *cute*. I wish I could take a photo of you right now."

She lobbed a piece of pizza crust at him and it bounced off his forehead and he jumped in surprise. "Less of the 'sweet and cute enough for a photo,' please. I'm a crack shot. Even with pizza crust. Don't mess with me."

He smiled and held up his hands. "Okay, so work or sleep?"

"Sleep, please. I think I need a taxi, though, or I'll have to sleep on the cot here."

"I'll call you a cab. You're a cab."

"So funny. So, so funny, old man." She gathered her things as he spoke fluent Greek to the taxi company they used fairly regularly for deliveries.

As she was being driven home, a lightness seeped into her soul. Maybe Simon hadn't been using her as a mark, so much as using his skills to get to know her, for him. Not for some mission. She wondered if she could ask him, but in doing so, she'd reveal her own training. She was in no position to ask him to be honest with her.

She fell straight on her bed when she got home, only just remembering to kick off her shoes as sleep washed over her. A calm, sweet sleep for the first time in ages.

CHAPTER SIXTEEN

The sun rose long before Simon did. He thought searching her room would reassure him. And it had temporarily. But again, these nagging doubts were back, invading his sleep, making him toss and turn until just before dawn.

He woke just before seven to find Mal had broken into his room again and was making coffee. "What the fuck?"

"Sorry, mate. I had a slight altercation with my coffee machine earlier. So I had to use yours."

"Have you heard of room service?"

"I don't like people coming in my room. I don't like anyone in my room. I don't even get it serviced. Which sucks when I'm on a job for weeks at a time, but I'm not big on sharing private space with anyone."

"But you think I am?" He hated this guy. Simon was always at a disadvantage when Garrett broke in like this, since he slept naked. He'd have to start sleeping in his clothes. Or he could booby-trap the hotel door. Yeah—that sounded more fun.

"Oh, take a pill. Anyone ever tell you how cranky you are in the morning?" He slurped his coffee and made himself at home in "his" armchair again.

"If you fucking made me a cup of coffee first, maybe I wouldn't be. Did you think of that?"

Garrett took another slurp. "Nope. Anyway, since when did you start sleeping in?"

When my ex-fiancée began screwing with my head. "Stamov stayed with girlfriend number two for a long time." Simon stifled a laugh. "I had to make a wrong-number call to his hotel room to wake his wife, who realized he wasn't there and called him to come home. It was the only way I figured I was getting any sleep at all. The horny bastard."

Garrett laughed. "Ballsy move. Okay, that deserves a coffee."

"Why don't you drink tea, anyway? I thought you Brits were all about your tea."

He rolled his eyes. "Yeah, and it's always foggy in London."

"Isn't it?" Ha. He'd found Garrett's weak spot.

"Fuck off."

"God save the Queen."

"La Marseillaise," he replied. At Simon's frown, he said, "Oh, sorry—I thought we were just randomly naming national anthems."

"Fuck off."

"Okay, so now we've got our morning hard-ons for each other out of the way. We need to start making plans, right?"

Simon couldn't help but grin. Garrett was an annoying bastard but no more annoying than the others on his team. And where the fuck were they? "I need to speak to Barnum. My team was supposed to be here last week. There is something wrong with that."

"Do you need me to leave?" Garrett asked, suddenly all business.

"Nope. He hired you. You're a part of this cluster whether you like it or not," Simon said, sliding into his jeans, trying not to give Garrett an eyeful. He reached across the bed and opened the laptop he'd inadvertently slept next to after he'd seen the minister back to the hotel.

He clicked on the video call icon and then his boss's name. At the last minute he realized that he was video calling his boss from his bed with no shirt on. He grabbed the PC and threw it gently to Garrett just as Barnum picked up.

"Tennant? Who is that?"

Simon quickly shrugged on a T-shirt and grabbed the PC back. "Sorry, sir; that's Malone Garrett from Barracks Security."

"Right. Good man, your boss," he said, sounding a little tinny through the speaker.

"Thank you, sir," Garrett said, embarrassed, shrugging at Simon from behind the computer screen.

"Do we have an ETA on my team, sir?"

"No, son. They've gotten as far as Albania. They were put on an EU watch list a couple of days ago, so we have the office there putting together fake passports. Something strange is happening there, Tennant. This has never happened before. But whatever it is, we will get them to you as soon as possible. The more barriers go up, the more determined we all are to get them to you. Understand?"

"Yessir." None of that made his heart sing with the joys of spring.

"Have you worked out a plan yet?" Even though the line was secure, his boss was obviously still being careful.

"We should have it finalized by this evening, sir. Do you want a report...or...?"

"No. Not necessary. I'll get the details when you come back." Typical Barnum. A good guy, a trustworthy guy, but he was all about the plausible deniability.

"Copy that, sir." Barnum reached forward and the screen went dark.

"By this evening, huh? I guess we better get on that," Garrett said, already starting another pot of coffee.

Simon nodded. At least it would be a busy day in which he wouldn't be thinking about Sadie. Unlike his dreams.

* * *

Sadie forced herself to get up early so that she had time to cover up any kind of appearance of a hangover. The pizza hadn't helped. She felt as if grease were pushing out of her pores.

As she went to turn the shower on, she heard a pinging that she hadn't heard before. She checked her company iPhone, her PC, and her two burner phones. None of them were beeping. And then she remembered. She'd set up the motion-detecting video camera to notify her after it had been activated. Her heart raced. Someone had been in her apartment?

She booted up her laptop and clicked on the secure-feed

icon. A color video stream of her apartment came up, with her sitting on her bed looking at the video feed. She hit the LAST ACTIVATION button. The screen went dark and the "buffering" progress crept across the screen.

"Come on, come on, come on," she breathed at its impossibly slow progress. Things are never as user-friendly as they seemed in the movies.

The screen changed to the recorded video, but just as the door opened and the footage showed a leg, it froze, buffering again. *Gahhh!* She resisted the temptation to throw the damn thing at the wall.

After a couple of minutes it started again, this time playing smoothly. It was Simon. Relief flooded through her, but a tension remained. It wasn't some unknown person touching her things, but it was someone who still obviously suspected her of...*oh my God.*

He was looking at her bedside table. He picked up her vibrator, and she watched as he jumped and started juggling it back into the drawer like it was a snake. She was mortified but couldn't help but giggle at his shock.

He moved around the room methodically until he sat on her bed and—what was he doing? Was he smelling her pillow? Warmth spread through her as she watched his chest heave in and out as if he couldn't get enough of her scent. Well, it was either that or he was trying to smother himself in a rather inefficient way.

Damn it—she wished she had a zoom lens on the camera. His hand was in his lap, and he looked like he was trying to rearrange himself. She pressed her hand to her mouth. But when he stood up, his erection was pretty clear.

He paused as he left, taking one last look around the room as if trying to memorize it. She was overwhelmed with warmth for him. Yes, he'd been searching her room, very efficiently. And yes, he obviously still had—correctly—doubts about her, but seeing him smell her pillow made a part of him—his non-covert-ops part—seem vulnerable to her. She wanted to see more of that part of him. More honesty, more openness. She wanted to really look in his eyes to see if what he said was real, what she felt was real. She put her PC down and clenched her fists. If she opened them, she would reach for her phone and write to the email address she'd been ignoring for months.

Instead she saved the video file—she was sure she'd want to watch it again—and took a shower before heading into work. She was the first at the office, so she got started reading the incoming telexes before getting back to checking all the people at the hotel when the incriminating email was sent. It was probably a fool's errand, because so many people could walk into a hotel and use its Internet in the public places...and that gave her an idea. She remembered that most hotels she'd been to had a separate password for people staying there. Maybe Stephanie could figure out whether it was a public-space Wi-Fi signal or a guest-room one. She wrote herself a note and went back to the list of names.

By the time Sebastian came in, she'd made herself some of his coffee and changed the number on the whiteboard to sixteen. He looked at it and grunted. "Great."

"Are you okay? You look a little green." She made a sympathetic face. "Do you want me to make you a cup of tea?"

"You're fine?" He rubbed his stomach again. "I thought it was the pizza."

"I woke up a little fragile, but I think that was the bourbon. Why don't you lie down on the cot until you feel better? I've been through the telexes and there's nothing there. I'm still sifting through the list of hotel guests, but I have an idea that might cut that down a bit too. Go lie down, and I'll come get you if anything needs your attention."

Sebastian got up. "Okay," he said weakly.

Sadie was worried. She hadn't known him that long, but generally men in operational jobs didn't admit there was anything wrong with them even if they'd been shot. She watched him go, making a mental note to call Netta later if he wasn't better.

The external phone rang. Her head snapped toward it and then to watch Sebastian disappear around the corner. He didn't even look back and frown at the call. He really didn't like anyone using the "cover company" phones unless it was an emergency, and the fact that her mark had discovered the phone number and kept calling...well, if nothing came of this Platon and Stratigos thing, she was going to look like an idiot and be branded her whole career as the one who made the newbie mistakes. She wouldn't be able to bear it if her father found out either.

The fake receptionist picked it up and put it through to her. "Hello, Inventory Management," she said in a singsong voice as if she'd been saying it for years.

"*Koukla mou*! I've missed you." Platon's voice sounded normal again after his split lip.

She lowered her voice as if her boss were listening. "How *are* you? You sound better."

"I'm fine. We need a favor. A big one. We will pay you lots of money. Are you interested?"

"Of course. What is it?" Her heart kicked up a notch.

"Stratigos did some research about your company, and he says you have a warehouse in Piraeus near the docks."

"Yes, we do. We only use it for storage, though. No one really goes there unless one of our sites needs something in an emergency." What were they going to do? A frisson of excitement shot through her.

"We just need the key for a night so that we can store something in there for a couple of days. Stratigos says he will give you three thousand euros."

Sadie's eyes flitted toward the corner that Sebastian had disappeared around. They did have a warehouse, but it just had a bunch of fake construction supplies in it—a digger, some pallets of cement, cinder blocks, and a lot of timber. It was there for customs inspections that happened once a year or anyone looking into property that Devries held. She needed to get down there first to see if it was still looking like a construction warehouse.

She lowered her voice even more. "Sure. Shall I meet you down there? Maybe at midday?"

There was mumbling off the phone, and then he came back. "That will be perfect."

She hung up and found the key to the warehouse in the chief's office. An icy finger of dread pressed up her spine, making her cold even in the humid office. What was she doing?

She was so far out of her depth she had no idea how to get herself out, except by being right about Platon and Stratigos. Was it horrible to hope they were hoping to create mayhem so that she could stop them?

Yes, yes it was. Shit.

Why couldn't she have just done the job they'd wanted her to do? Be nice to people, buy drinks, expand her social network so that she had access to many different types of people for gathering intelligence. Instead, she'd gotten a complete hard-on for the one guy she found suspicious and hadn't really done much to get to know anyone else. She hadn't even followed up on the weird thumb drive that she'd retrieved—or stolen—from the director's office before.

She'd passed the point of no return now. She had to keep going. And if her instincts were right, she'd prove she'd earned this job, not just been handed the assignment because her father was the director.

But she was damned if she was going to get Sebastian involved in this mess too. At least not until she had some kind of hard evidence to show him.

She grabbed her bag and left the office with the key. She got a couple of copies made and then hustled back to the office to return the original to the station chief's office.

But instead of going to her desk, she went up one further flight of creaky stairs and used a keypad to enter her own individual passcode. Despite the old building they were in, the door opened smoothly as if it were on a hydraulic mechanism. For all she knew, it was. When she'd first been shown this room, she could barely suppress the feeling of being in *Mission*

Impossible or something. Nothing really to do with the contents of the room—just the door. She sighed. She was kind of sad.

She used her phone to scan the barcode on a black acrylic backpack that held surveillance equipment and then the barcode on a large ziplock bag that had a wig in it. Well, there was no getting around the fact that she was logging out this equipment, so she was going to be found out eventually; she just hoped that she'd have something to show for it by the time it happened. She snagged some clothing items from the hooks along the wall and left the room.

In the ladies' room she changed into some jeans and work boots, tucked her hair into the short, dark wig, and put on one of her old, raggedy T-shirts she kept at the office in case she needed to sleep there. She slung her purse across her chest and pulled on the backpack. She attached a hard hat to the backpack. No one would question her going into the Devries warehouse at the docks. There was even a Devries logo on the hat.

Now she had to get there and set everything up in less than an hour.

CHAPTER SEVENTEEN

W ell, it's not looking good for your bird," Garrett said over his earpiece. He and Simon had come to a kind of peace treaty, where they would split covering the minister and Sadie between them. Simon wondered how long Garrett would agree to that, how long it would be before she got herself into some kind of trouble that needed their intervention.

He'd been watching Stamov and planning the best way to exfiltrate him. "What's not looking good? I thought you were having brunch?" Simon smiled to himself. Of all the people he'd ever met, Garrett was the least likely to even know what brunch was, let alone go get some.

"Very funny, G.I. Joe. I'm talking about your girl. Unless she's given her purse to someone, which I understand women rarely do, she is in the port of Piraeus, making her way through containers and shipments and a lot of dockworkers who are swinging around to get a better look at her."

What the fuck? He tried to think of a reason she'd be

there. Truth was, no matter how he felt about her emotionally, he didn't know anything about her life here now.
Seriously nothing. Maybe she had a book club at the docks.
Or maybe there was a consignment sale. He shook his head
as the thoughts occurred to him. He really needed to get to
know her better if he had any chance with her again. "Give
me a minute, dude."

"Sure, sure," Garrett said.

Simon did a Google Maps search for Devries Construction.
The map showed an office in the city and one at the docks. As
he zoomed in, he could see it was a warehouse. Okay. So she
was there for work.

"Garrett. Her company has a warehouse at the port. It's
okay. She must be there for some work thing."

There was silence. "Garrett?" He heard two taps on the earpiece, meaning he couldn't talk.

His mind set at rest, Simon went back to his plan. Whoever
was going to take the Russian finance minister and blame it
on the US, well—he wasn't going to let them get away with it.
There were sixteen days until the president landed, so he suspected something would go down either way before he even
boarded Air Force One.

"Tennant. Sorry, she walked right past my position. What
were you saying?" Garrett asked.

"Her company has a warehouse in the port area. I'm sure it's
no problem."

"Hmm," he replied.

"What do you mean 'hmm'?" His mind was still on the
plan. Maybe they could force the plan to be executed earlier.

Garrett could offer to take the minister away somewhere he couldn't resist, maybe.

"If that were the case, why do you think she'd be wearing a disguise?"

That got his attention. He frowned. "You mean like dark-glasses-and-a-hat kind of disguise?"

"Nope. I mean like disguised like a man. A short-haired wig, a hard hat, glasses. Thing is, no matter how she's trying, she cannot hide that crazy body. Am I right?"

"Get your eyes off her body. I'm coming to you. Give me your position." Stamov seemed to be entrenched in a meeting that wasn't due to end for hours. And worst case, Simon could locate him with the tracker if need be.

Ten minutes later, he was on the move. The Metro gave the cleanest straight shot to the port, and the cars were largely empty save for backpackers heading to the port for one of the many ferries that operate between Athens and the Greek islands.

He tried to order his thoughts. She was in disguise? She must be doing something for her ridiculous boyfriend. If you could call him that. He certainly didn't. Fuck lifting the finance minister; he was ready to lift Sadie and keep her until she came to her senses about that man.

By the time he reached the port, Garrett was sitting on a concrete trash can, eating a Greek kebab, presumably from the nearby food truck, and drinking a bottle of beer.

"What the fuck are you doing? You're supposed to be following her." He wanted to punch through the man's Ray-Bans and rip his brain out.

Garrett took another bite and nodded toward a building. He chewed, swallowed, took a sip of beer, and then said, "She's still in there. Whoops. Speak of the devil."

Simon looked at the doorway and saw Sadie locking it. She looked perfectly normal. "What disguise?" He turned his back on her so she wouldn't notice him.

"Nah, I just said that to make you come down for...brunch." Garrett smiled for about two seconds, just long enough for Simon to make a reach for him. He ducked out of the way. "Kidding, mate. She changed while she was in there. Oh, fuck. Don't look now but she's not going anywhere; she looks like she's waiting for someone. Do you want to head over there, out of her direct sight line so we can get a proper look?"

Simon snatched his beer away from him so it looked like they were just workers stopped for a break as they walked slowly away. Neither of them looked back; neither seemed as if he was in a hurry.

As soon as they rounded the side of a shipping container, they stopped, back to its metal wall. Simon nodded skyward, and Garrett, to his credit, didn't ask questions. He bent his knee so Simon could climb up, using his knee and then his shoulder to get enough height to pull himself onto the roof of the container. Fuck, it was hot—like burning hot. Simon could feel the heat through his shoes. He quietly lay down and shuffled to the far edge, trying to ignore the burning. He'd been in more painful stakeouts. Not many, but some.

Something soft landed on his legs. Garrett's jacket. Simon grabbed it and tucked it under his elbows to relieve the scorching heat. It was kind of like Garrett was part of his team already. They'd always been taught to anticipate one another's needs on an op, and he guessed that Garrett had received similar training somewhere in the UK.

His gaze didn't leave Sadie. She paced up and down in front of the door, checking her watch occasionally and looking toward the entrance. Then five men appeared from the opposite direction she'd been expecting. As she turned at the end of her pacing path, she was startled to see them. Suddenly he wanted to be in a more accessible place in case she needed him. He saw movement out of his peripheral vision and turned slightly to see Garrett pressed against the opposite container, sleeves rolled up and waiting for an instruction.

He pointed at Garrett's eyes with two fingers, then at his own, and then at the meeting going on, telling him that Simon would watch Sadie and give the signal if he needed Garrett to intervene. He responded with a sharp nod and stayed back to the wall, watching only Simon.

Simon made a mental note to ease up on him. He was obviously a stellar soldier. Of course, the heavily redacted file Barnum sent him didn't give any information on any military service, but Garrett was too good not to be military.

Simon watched Sadie hug her "boyfriend" briefly, causing bile to rise in his throat. She held his hand while passing the older guy something small and taking an envelope in return. He kissed her on both cheeks, and Simon sensed rather than saw her recoil. Interesting dynamic. She really didn't like the older guy. But that didn't necessarily mean anything—maybe he made a pass at her before?

Focus, dammit; focus on the mission. Except what kind of

mission was this? The mission to spy on his ex? Sadie kissed her "boyfriend" on the lips and walked away, back toward the entrance. The other five watched her leave, then looked at each other without saying anything and turned to the warehouse. The older guy unlocked it and the others filed in, Sadie's boyfriend only pausing to receive a pat on the back from the guy with the key.

So that's what Sadie gave him. The key. He would give anything to have eyes inside that warehouse. Anything. As soon as they all disappeared, he threw Garrett's jacket down and climbed down, jumping the last few feet.

"She gave the warehouse key to the anarchist group," he said, still watching the doorway.

"Well, that doesn't look good."

"No kidding. I want to see if there are any other access points—or windows, come to that." They made their way around the warehouse and found nothing that wasn't locked up tight. As they surveilled the rear of the warehouse, the giant doors started to slide slowly open. They bolted for opposite corners of the building. Nothing happened for a while, and Simon had to restrain himself from looking.

"Transport coming at your nine o'clock. Back up, back up." Garrett's voice came low and urgent over his earpiece.

Shit. He backed up to the front corner, trying to remain out of sight. "Do you have eyes on them?" he whispered back.

"Eyes and video. Give me a few minutes and I'll meet you at the food truck."

Simon retreated, squashing the thought that he wanted to hug that man. When they rendezvoused, they decided to bolt back to the hotel to make it in time for the end of Stamov's morning meeting. He had been known to ditch the afternoon meetings in favor of a girlfriend or two.

But one thing Simon knew. He had to see Sadie.

* * *

When Sadie retuned to the office, the street and doorway were swarming with civilians. If she hadn't recognized one of them from the embassy, she might have backed away and not seen the paramedics close up their doors and drive off.

She ran up the stairs two at a time. "What happened?" she asked the guy she knew who had beaten her back into the office.

"Where were *you*?" he replied with a frown.

What was his name? What was his...ha! She remembered: weak jaw—Shaw.

"I was out, Mr. Shaw. What happened?" She was getting annoyed, and she certainly wasn't cluing this bureaucrat in on her whereabouts.

"Sebastian Seeker's wife couldn't reach him. Not on his cell or on his office number, so she dropped by and found him unresponsive. A suspected heart attack."

Sadie's heart didn't just drop; it shriveled into a ball. Why hadn't she checked on him before she left? Maybe he was having a heart attack while she was still in the office and she just sneaked off, worried that he might stop her. "Will he be okay?" Her voice cracked on the last word.

"I have no idea. But I'm suspending all activity from this office until Lassiter returns or is replaced." He barely looked up from the phone he was typing into, but she saw his smirk. God help them if he was angling for the station chief job himself.

"Go home. Enjoy yourself; take a vacation. You'll be called when the office is reopened," he said.

This wasn't happening. She grabbed his sleeve and pulled him away from the paramedics. "You can't just close down the intelligence office sixteen days before the president comes. That's crazy. You have no idea—"

"Stop it right there, Ms. Walker. You will obey this order, and you will suspend any operation you are involved in. We'll all be back up and running soon." He stuffed his phone back in his pants pocket and shot his cuffs. "This ridiculous outfit has seen its day. High time Lassiter was put out to pasture, anyway." He gestured around the room. "This mess is typical of his leadership, or lack of."

Concentrate, Sadie. Don't waste your time here; you can break back in anytime you want.

"I'm going to the hospital to sit with Netta. If you need me..."

"I won't. Leave your office keys with Darnish at the door." He gave her a tight grin and turned away, all but dismissing her. She assumed Darnish was the fresh-faced guy in the button-down. He smiled and held a box out to her. Inside were a set of keys and Sebastian's ID. She clenched her fist as she dropped her own in alongside. Fucking Shaw had fucking *frisked* Sebastian before he left for the hospital. There was no reason for that. Their CIA magnetized IDs were actually branded with their cover companies, so hers said Devries Construction. There was absolutely no reason to take them.

"Shaw needs you," she said as she made to leave. As soon as Darnish started walking into the other room, she snagged the diplomatic pouch from the hook by the door. The pouch allowed them to send things to other countries without the local governments being allowed to look in them. She had an idea about the forgotten thumb drive.

She ran out of the office and hailed a cab to the hospital. Her stomach was rolling at the thought of what she'd done to Sebastian. *Please let him have been okay when I left.* How would she be able to look Netta in the face?

She rushed in and was directed to Intensive Care. Netta was there, white faced and rigid in her seat.

"Netta."

She rose and at the sight of Sadie, her shoulders slumped. "Thank you for coming, darling."

Sadie hugged her, trying not to show the terror and desperation she felt. "How is he?"

"Still unconscious. Hooked up to a million machines. I just don't know."

They held hands and sat in silence, only looking up when nurses and doctors walked by, just in case they had some information. They never did.

CHAPTER EIGHTEEN

When Garrett told him that Sadie's tracker was absolutely still in a private hospital, Simon couldn't stay away. He tasked Garrett with keeping an eye on the minister and headed out into the night.

What was Sadie doing in the hospital? Was she hurt? Sick? Had that bastard done something to her? Would he ever forgive himself if he'd stood by while that had happened?

Taking deep breaths of the humid air to stop him from freaking the fuck out, he found a taxi and folded himself into the back of the small car. The taxi driver looked concerned when he said he wanted the hospital and started playing with his prayer beads as he drove. Simon appreciated the thought.

The driver went slow enough that he didn't feel like he needed to urge him on and fast enough that he wasn't also in fear of his own life. As they pulled up, he shoved a fifty-euro note to the man—for the prayers—and leapt from the car. He was about to run in through the sliding doors to the

ER when he saw her, leaning against a pillar, smoking.

Relief flooded through him. Proper, real relief, making his legs weak and his blood pound back the adrenaline he was using as fuel. He took a few deep breaths and headed toward her.

As he got closer, he could see her hands shaking each time she brought the cigarette up to her mouth. She wasn't even inhaling—no surprise, really, because she didn't smoke.

"Sadie?" he asked in a manner that he hoped would imply that he wasn't expecting to see her. "Why are you smoking?"

She looked around, and when her eyes met his, her face held steady for a couple of seconds—long enough to say, "I bummed it from a nurse; even the nurses smoke"—and then it crumpled. He was beside her in a second, arms holding her tight. "What happened?" Now that she was safe in his arms, he was able to inhale the scent of her shampoo without detection, the very same scent that had given him an erection while he was searching her room.

"My friend died. My work colleague. It was my fault. I should have been there," she sobbed into his shoulder. He held her tighter to try to squeeze her sobs back in.

He hailed the same taxi that hadn't moved from the spot where Simon had left it. He gave the man Sadie's address and put her in the car. She wasn't responsive—it was like she was going into shock or just couldn't compute what had happened. He'd seen her like this before, in Mumbai, where they'd met. He knew how her emotions would progress.

Sliding his arm around her, he held her as tightly as he could against him. He wanted to think that he was being of comfort to her, but the truth was he was a bastard. He just liked feeling her this close to his body. Liked feeling the heat of her, even in this unholy hellhole-hot climate.

He hated that she was sad, but if that made her compliant and noncombative, well, he was going to take advantage of that. He *was* a bastard. What the hell was he thinking? He wasn't going to do any of that. Those days had passed.

The cab driver refused to take any money from him, which definitely had Sadie doing a double take, so he slipped them both out and up to her apartment. He took her key from her, opened the door, and she went in.

He hovered in the doorway. "Do you want me to come in?"

* * *

Her brain barely registered the question, but a flashback to Mumbai shook her. Familiar anger bubbled up, and she let it—it felt so much better than fear, and sadness, and aching regret, and guilt. Anger was positive.

But she wasn't supposed to be angry anymore. She knew that men used their skills to meet women. Sebastian had told her. Pain pierced her chest with the thought. Sebastian.

She held her hand to her chest and took a breath. And another, and she still couldn't get enough air in her lungs. She started heaving and her panicked eyes met Simon's.

In a second she was on the floor, breathing into a white paper bag. He held it to her mouth, and she struggled against it for a second, thinking he was trying to suffocate her. And then the pain in her lungs eased, and they seemed to inflate with enough oxygen to breathe.

"It's okay. You're just hyperventilating. Relax and exhale for as long as you can."

She nodded and he pulled the bag away.

"Better?"

She nodded again, closed her eyes, and sat back against the bed. Moments later, she felt him sit next to her.

"Here," he said.

She opened her eyes and found an icy bottle of Grey Goose in front of her face. "How did you...?"

He shook it. "I know you, Sadie. You always have a bottle in your freezer, even when you have no food in the house." He half laughed.

She took the bottle and swigged a mouthful before handing it back. Simon did the same.

"We used to only need a bottle of vodka to have a great evening. That beats having a full fridge," she said, prolonging the moments before she knew she'd have to think, and maybe talk, about Sebastian.

"That's true. The guys at work called it the 'Sadie Diet': vodka, sex, and late nights." He passed the bottle back again.

She knew he was joking, but it still sounded bad. "I was a bad girlfriend, I guess. I should have cooked for you more." A healthy slug of vodka made her suck in cooling air between her teeth. Maybe she was just bad at everything. Her job, being a girlfriend—her mind skipped to Sebastian—being a human. She wanted to prove that she was good at one thing. She knew she should go check the warehouse camera feeds, but she just didn't have the energy or the inclination. The excitement she'd felt at her "operation" seemed so distant to her, like it had happened years before...and to someone else.

"You were a great girlfriend. If I'd wanted food, I'd have cooked for myself." He took a hit from the bottle again. "That never even crossed my mind. In fact, I wondered..."

"Wondered what?"

"Wondered if it had been *my* fault. I should have been more of...I don't know. A stable person in your life. Looking back, it felt like when I was with you, it was just for a fleeting visit. I was always traveling, always having to apologize for not being around. Always leaving you."

She suddenly realized in the haze of vodka and guilt and sorrow that they'd never, ever talked about their relationship. Not when they were in it, and not when they finished it. This wasn't the way to get closure, and it wasn't the way to mourn a friend.

"I think I need to go home, back to the States. Probably. Someone from headquarters shut the office after Sebastian was taken to the hospital. I'm not sure I even have a job. And they pay for this apartment." She hiccupped. "And even if they didn't fire me, I'm not sure I could go back and sit opposite the empty desk where he used to sit." She tried to hold back her tears. No sobbing. She didn't deserve the outlet, the catharsis.

With his thumbs Simon wiped tears she didn't know were there. "I don't think you should make any decisions tonight, sweetheart. Come on." He stood and held his hand out for her. She took it and he pulled her up. "Let's just sleep on it. See how you feel in the morning." He started unbuttoning his shirt and shucking off his shoes. "Don't look at me like that.

I'm just staying to make sure you're all right." Lines furrowed his brow.

She acquiesced for a second and then remembered why she had hated him all this past year. "No. No, you don't get to do that again. Be the honorable guy, sneak out in the morning, leaving your number on the bedside table. You are in, or you're out."

"I don't—"

She started unbuttoning her blouse, and when that was done, she unzipped her skirt. "In or out?" She placed her hands on her hips and waited for his reply.

"In," he said softly.

He paused for a second and then took one step so that she had to crane her neck to look at him. He smoothed the hair from her face and lowered his face to hers. The intensity blazing in his eyes took her breath away. His kiss kicked her rational mind to the sidelines. Her tongue kept pace with his, plundering his mouth, tasting his breath as he was doing hers.

There was nothing but him. His hands on her. His mouth on her. Yes. Screw the honorable Simon. She'd take this one every day of the week for the rest of her life. An alarm bell rang in her head as that thought passed through her mind, but it evaporated as fast as her panties and bra had under Simon's skillful hands.

"Are you sure?" he asked, hesitating in an uncharacteristic way.

She took a small step back and indicated her naked body. "What part of this says I'm not sure?"

He laughed and pulled her against him for another knee-melting kiss. Blood rushed through her at the speed of light, making everything on the outside of her seem like it was moving in slow motion.

He picked her up and threw her on the bed, making her gasp and bounce so hard that she nearly fell off the other side. His own shocked face was a picture. She laughed. And then giggled. "You totally thought I'd wiped out there, didn't you?"

He smiled. "I thought I'd lost you for good. The damned bed's more bouncy than I remember."

She was about to say something, but as he undid his belt and jeans, her mind stuttered at the sight of Simon, naked and excited. She held her hand out to him.

In a second he lay alongside her, trailing the back of his fingers down her body from her neck to her thigh. Up again and down again. Her nipples hardened and goosebumps erupted as his fingers lazily swirled around her skin.

She stretched under his fingers, enjoying the feeling of taut skin under his fingertips.

"I've missed you," he said in a low voice.

Her eyes met his, but she said nothing. She couldn't properly process the right thing to say, not when his hands were lighting her on fire.

"I've missed this."

That she could concur with. "Me too." She turned on her side and put a hand on his hard chest. "Tell me exactly what you've missed, Mr. Tennant," she said.

He didn't hesitate. He held his hand over her breast and only allowed the very middle of his palm to lightly touch her nipple. "I've missed the expression on your face when your whole body is begging for more of a touch." He licked his fingers and touched her nipple, blowing on it immediately after. A cool burn shot from her breasts to her stomach and down her legs.

She arched her back, wanting to feel more of him.

"I've missed the sound you make in your throat when I touch you here." Without hesitation, or foreplay, or anything, his finger settled directly on her clitoris.

She jumped and moaned, eliciting a smile from Simon.

"Exactly. Open your legs," he said.

She spread them instantly, giving him more access. She was so ready for him, so hot and wet; she could feel blood rushing and pulsing through her.

"I've missed how obedient you are too," he said.

She pinched his arm but couldn't bring herself to move away from the delicious circles his fingers were drawing.

He pressed his whole hand against her, the heel of his hand against her clit and his fingers playing, feeling her, until one slid inside her.

She bucked against his hand, but he easily held her in place.

He dipped his head and touched the tip of his tongue to the nipple closest to him, then he was sucking and biting as his fingers drafted across her clitoris, taking her in seconds to the point of orgasm and then slipping inside her again and then back to drive her even closer.

"I want you inside me, Simon," she said, suddenly needing his weight on hers, his body touching every part of hers. She'd missed that. The feeling of utter safety and protection. The feeling that his body pressing down on hers was somehow anchoring her to his world, his life.

She arched her hips against his and he slid on top of her, bracing himself on his elbows, his hands cradling her face. She turned her head to kiss one of his hands as he pushed slowly inside her. She gasped and bit her lip, in part to keep her jaw from hanging slack at the friction caused by his movements. With each thrust, her brain said *home, home, home.*

He stopped while he was deep inside her and rolled onto his side, taking her with him. It was like they were joined from their thighs to their mouths. They breathed in each other's mouths as they kissed, his fingers digging into the leg that was over his, pulling it farther over his hip. His hand slipped between them, and he found her clitoris with one finger and swirled around it in her wetness.

Simon pulled away from her mouth and set his jaw. Sadie knew he was trying not to come, but the thought of him holding back sent her skittering toward the edge of her own orgasm. She was hungry for it, hungry for him. She rocked her pelvis against his as the heat of the pulse of fire ebbed and flowed in her body until it spread like a slow-moving tsunami. She gasped with the force of her release, clenching her muscles around him, pulsing as the flood inside her dissipated.

He came almost immediately afterward, shuddering against her, breathing her name as he did.

She felt loved. Complete. But in the warmth of the afterglow, she had no idea if any of it was real.

For the first time, she hoped it was.

CHAPTER NINETEEN

When Simon awoke, he took a moment to watch Sadie sleep. Her skin reflected the small amount of light that the window allowed in, making her look as if she were a sleeping angel. He smiled. One with a filthy mind.

He could tell she was the same Sadie he'd asked to marry him, but in so many respects she was totally different. Changed in a way that sometimes people do within a relationship, he supposed. Maybe if they'd stayed together, she would have changed in exactly the same way.

Rolling on his back and staring at the ceiling, he wondered if he should tell her that he wanted her back in his life. Wondered if it was too big of an ask. She'd have to leave Greece, settle somewhere, and be prepared for at least another three to five years of him rarely being around much. And that seemed to be the key problem. Question was, did he love Sadie as much as he loved his job? Would he give up Delta Force for her? He'd have to make that decision before he broached the subject of them getting back together.

He wanted to wake her, to talk to her, to do unspeakable things to her. But he knew that as soon as she was awake, sober, she would remember that her friend was dead. She needed to sleep as long as she could.

His phone bleeped. Dammit. He reached for it before it could ring again and disturb her.

Too late. She rolled onto her back and stretched. Her eyes opened and her gaze rested on him. She smiled and closed her eyes again, and then they shot open a second before she sat upright.

She remembered.

He glanced at his phone. It was Garrett with a 911 text message. He needed to go. But leaving Sadie was torture.

She put her face into her hands. "Oh God. It wasn't a dream, was it? Sebastian died, didn't he?"

He stroked her back. "I'm afraid so. And as much as I want to stay and talk to you, I really have to go. I've been here too—" Pain pierced his heart as he realized that he was doing what he'd always done.

She waved her hand. "It's okay. I understand."

He knew she did. But he also knew that they'd had too many moments like this in the year or so they'd been together. Him having to leave for one operational crisis or another, whether or not she was hurt, happy, sad, or just tired. He felt like he'd already missed years of sharing in her emotions. In that minute, he realized that he could leave CAG for her. Would. There were other people who could do his job, but only he could love Sadie as much as he did.

He pulled on his pants and sat next to her on the bed. "I'll come back tonight and we can have dinner and talk about everything that's worrying you right now, okay?" He held her hand and looked for her acquiescence. He wanted to say "and make plans," but he didn't. He didn't have time to explain that part to her now. She nodded and squeezed his hand, not meeting his eyes.

He donned his T-shirt, grabbed his phone again, and kissed her on top of her head, holding his lips there for a second. "Sorry," he said again, against her hair.

"Sure," she said, sounding distant.

Shit. He'd have some making up to do tonight. And the rest of all the nights ever.

He couldn't help but grin as he shut the door behind him. Being absolutely sure about his future was rare, and he intended to enjoy every second of it.

It took him barely ten minutes to run back to the hotel. Even in the heat of the early morning, he felt lighter and freer than usual. It was going to be a great day. Whatever happened, if he ended his day with Sadie, it was going to be a great day.

"What's up?" he said as he closed the hotel room door behind him. He didn't bother registering surprise that Garrett was in his room again. Clearly the term "personal space" didn't translate into the Queen's English.

He was looking at the room service menu. "Which should I have—the sausages or the yogurt-and-honey thing?"

"Please tell me that wasn't your nine-one-one emergency." He threw his phone on the bed and went to the bathroom to switch on the shower.

"Well, sometimes it's difficult to know how best to set up your day for success, you know, mate?"

Simon's happy, great-day feeling started to fray around the edges. He poked his head out from the bathroom. "And I say again: Please tell me your breakfast choices weren't the subject of your nine-one-one text." So help him, he would flush that bastard's head down the toilet if it was.

He put the menu down. "Nope, but I'm betting that in a few minutes, you'll prefer my breakfast to be your emergency. Take a look at that." He threw his phone to Simon, who caught it one-handed, just preventing it from ending up in the bottom of the shower.

"What am I looking at?" he asked as he swiped into the iPhone.

"Last night's photos," Garrett replied, holding his hand over the mouthpiece of the room phone. "One bottle of champagne—" He looked at Simon and raised his eyebrows in question. Then shrugged. "Two glasses. Orange juice, sausages, eggs, and your yogurt-and-honey thing too. Yup, charge it to the room."

"That's coming out of your fee, you know," Simon said, leaning against the frame of the door to the bathroom.

"No, it won't. It will miraculously be wiped from your mind in five, four, three—"

"Oh shit. *Shit.*" Simon felt the lightheartedness of his morning sink into a hot tar pit of hell as he viewed the pics on Garrett's phone.

"And there you have it. Yes, mate. Shit indeed."

He skimmed through the photos of the Russian finance minister leaving the hotel where he visited mistress number two, not with the mistress, but with the old man he'd seen with Sadie at the warehouse. Her boyfriend's uncle, allegedly. Hell, he hadn't even gotten to the bottom of that either. Did she really consider that boy as her boyfriend? She couldn't, could she? There was no way the Sadie he knew would sleep with two men concurrently. Doubt seeped into his brain and obliterated any remaining happiness he'd felt this morning. Thing is, he didn't know her now.

Getting his head back on the mission, he sat on the end of the bed and accepted a silently proffered cup of coffee. He continued to flip through the photos of the two men inside the hotel, talking. Then he came to a candid photo of a stunning woman with long, light blond hair, smiling at something beyond the camera, her hair blowing around her head in the breeze. He handed the phone back to Garrett. "Really?"

He looked at the photo and smiled. "Not what you think, mate."

Simon didn't really care. "It looks from the photos that they didn't want to be linked together outside the hotel. I mean, they seemed to be chatting inside the hotel, but as soon as they exited they went in different directions and didn't acknowledge each other. Does that feel right?"

"That's my impression, yes. I followed him to the hotel, figured as it was his second stop of the day, I might be waiting for over an hour. So I got a drink at the bar and waited. Before I'd even finished my second drink, they came down together in the lift. I got a photo of the doors as they opened, because I was actually trying to get a photo of a woman at the other end of the bar."

Simon rolled his eyes and sighed.

"Hey, if I hadn't, we wouldn't even have a clue that these two knew each other and may have been meeting each other all this time," he protested.

"Whatever. So you think there was never a second mistress? I followed her in to the hotel on her first day in the country and watched her check in."

"She was there. But she checked out the following day and flew home. At least the bellboy told me he put her in a taxi to the airport. I suspect he's been meeting this guy all along."

"What's his name?" Garrett asked.

Simon pulled up a secure file on his PC. "Geronimo Anton. Also known as 'Stratigos.' Responsible for car bombings, stabbings, and some firebombing in his youth. A known anarchist, in and out of prison. But obviously out now."

"So why would Stamov be mixing it up with an anarchist? What could they possibly have to talk about?" Garrett asked.

"Could it be that he's heard about the abduction rumors and has enlisted Stratigos's help to protect him?" Simon said.

"I've been following him for most of the time that I haven't been drinking with him, and I haven't seen anyone on watch or anyone surveilling him except his own Russian bodyguards. So that probably isn't it."

A knock at the door interrupted them. Room service. He let the waiter set up, and Garrett tipped him well...on the check. More money added to Simon's room bill. He sighed, but he couldn't bring himself to care too much. He picked up a sausage and ate it with his fingers as he thought, resisting the urge to lick all the other sausages so that Garrett couldn't have any.

Except he had the distinct impression that not only would

that absolutely not bother Garrett, but that Simon might even go up a few notches in his estimation. How did he get stuck with such an immature jerk?

Then he remembered what a good operator he'd seemed at the docks and mentally shrugged. They were just different.

"So what's your take?" he asked, seeing if Garrett's brain was hardwired the same as his.

"The girlfriend checked in and out within a day. That was planned and means that the frequent stops at the hotel were planned, probably when he was still in Russia. So he'd already arranged to meet Stratigos and figured out a way to cover up the meetings. Given Russia's, uh, shall we say, 'assertiveness' in its dealings with other countries, I doubt they're putting together a surprise party for someone. Russia has long been offering to cover Greece's debt to the European Union in return for some latitude in building Russian military bases in the middle of Europe, and Stamov is the finance minister."

Simon agreed. "But why is he negotiating with anarchists instead of the government?" Simon honestly didn't have an answer to that one, but Garrett did.

"In some respects, Greek governments are kind of like Italian ones. Elections and referendums are fairly common. It wouldn't actually surprise me at all to find out Russia was funding a Soviet-friendly opposition to the incumbent government," he said.

"Why would Stamov have to meet him daily to agree to that?" Simon grabbed another sausage and finished it before he even really registered eating it. He wondered what Sadie was doing, and something pulled at his conscience. He should have stayed with her. Made sure she was okay.

"Guess I'm having the yogurt, then," Garrett said, making no move to eat anything. "But yes, taking meetings is very old school. Hiding them, though, is definitely some kind of subterfuge. It's all possible, but it sounds like a long con to me. Nothing that needs to be settled before a G20 meeting, or even at a G20 meeting. The timing is just off."

"You think it's about something that's going down now?"

"Stamov *is* involved in something going down now—his alleged abduction. What are the odds he's involved in two separate things? Could he be in on the kidnapping? Could it be a bait and switch?"

"God only knows. But our mission is to watch him and take him if it looks like he's about to be lifted," Simon said. His role really wasn't strategic like this. Both he and, he assumed, Garrett were point-and-shoot operatives. The mission is given and they carry it out. This not knowing exactly what was happening was a little out of his comfort zone.

Garrett put his cup down. "And not for nothing, you know that counterabduction is close to impossible with just the two of us, especially when one of us is off mooning over some girl and not concentrating on the job." He raised his eyebrows at Simon, no hint of sarcasm playing on his face.

Simon sighed. "I know. I know. But she's involved in this somehow. What would you do?"

"Me? If I were you, I'd get my excessively handsome partner-in-crime to occupy Stamov with wine, women, and song, while I go to my girl and make her tell me what the fuck is going on." He smiled a shit-eating smile that didn't make it to his eyes, or most of his face, for that matter.

"Fuck." Simon sat on the bed and buried his face in his hands. "Yeah. Yeah, you're right. Let's finish our planning, and then I'll go speak to her this afternoon." At least he could make sure she was okay after the death of her coworker. He clenched his fists. If only they could have spent time together without all the life-and-death stuff happening around them. Maybe then they would have had time to work it all out. Maybe then they'd already be married.

Maybe.

* * *

Sadie was at the airport, looking for the State Department courier who always took the midday flight to London and then went on to Paris before returning to his home base at the embassy in Rome.

She'd snagged the diplomatic pouch from the hook before Shaw had shut down the office, because she realized that Stephanie, the tech analyst in Paris, might be able to help her with the weird thumb drive she hadn't been able to figure out. The diplomatic pouches traveled daily between embassies and Washington, DC, as a part of an international agreement. No foreign government or customs or immigration could touch the diplomatic pouches when they were en route.

The courier walked in through the revolving doors, looking just like a regular tourist. She waved and he smiled and walked over.

"This is a happy coincidence," he said, holding out his hand. "Or is it? I went to the office and it was locked up. Everything okay?" He blew a section of his floppy surfer-style hair out of his eyes. Oh, if she were ten years younger.

Her heart twisted as she thought about Sebastian. "A colleague died yesterday. He had a heart attack right there in the office. She could feel her chin tremble, and she tried to hide it from the courier as well as herself.

"That's terrible. I'm so sorry. Is there anything I can do?" He put his small carry-on down and his brow furrowed. "How long will the office be closed?"

"Just for this week while we—" She choked a little, deliberately. "Until after his funeral." She felt horrible lying to him, but if he suspected that the office had been officially shut down for who knew how long, he would never accept her package. "I managed to grab our last dip pouch before we locked up shop. But I spent the night at the hospital, so I thought it was best to try and find you here."

"Of course, of course." He took the pouch from her, checked that it was locked, and put it in his bag. "You'll let me know when I can come pick up from the office again?" he asked, hefting the bag to his shoulder.

"I'll telex Rome first thing," she said with a weak smile.

He smiled with sympathy. "Chin up. As Churchill said, 'If you're going through hell, keep going.'" He took her hand to shake it and squeezed it just a little as he let go.

He was so nice. People were so nice—it was such a shame she had to lie to all of them. She took a second in the busy terminal to watch all the passengers moving like ants in a farm, letting her mind wander. She had to come to terms with the fact that her whole life was going to be a lie. She would have to tell lies to every person that she met, that she kissed. Her mind fluttered to Simon for the fiftieth time that morning. He had lied to her when he first met her, and only when she accepted his proposal did he come clean about his clandestine job.

He was supposed to wait until they were actually married, but he didn't. She wondered why. And he couldn't have chosen better when it came to secrecy. She'd been born into secrets and lies, with her father embedded deep in the CIA before he became its director.

She should call her dad, let him know what was going on here; maybe he could send help. She'd definitely call him.

Okay, getting the thumb drive to Stephanie was the first thing on her list. Check. Second thing was to try to get into the office security system without her ID card so that she could watch the footage of whatever happened in the warehouse. Thank God Shaw didn't know anything about the warehouse; otherwise, he would have shut that down too. And third, she'd call her father.

The fourth thing on her list might be vodka. She'd wait to see how she felt.

As she sat on the Metro back to the city, she figured she should just break into the office rather than try to hack in remotely. It was a far more time-efficient way of handling her problem. Besides which, she could grab the go-bag items she'd hidden from Simon.

In any event, the front door to the offices was open. One of the other tenants must have left it ajar for some reason. Which only left her with the two doors actually into their office on the top floor. Shaw, or one of his people, had helpfully put up tape that said "contamination" in Greek. Could be fleas, could be radiation, but she guessed it was enough to keep all but the hard-core criminals at bay.

She picked the lock with no problems and retrieved what remained of her go bag and her illegal weapon from her locker. Thankfully no one seemed to have checked anyone's personal lockers. Probably thought they were all as benign as they probably should have been.

She went back into the actual office and stopped for a moment to look at all the loose wiring where the computers used to be. In the kitchen, she saw that the fuckers had also stolen Sebastian's own coffee machine. She dug her nails into her palms as she gazed at the space where his beloved contraption had been. Utter. Bastards.

They'd taken a bunch of other things that were clearly nothing to do with national security too. Maybe that was one of the perks of their jobs. One day, if she came across them again, she would do them wrong. She gritted her teeth in determination and to try to stop herself from crying.

A phone rang in the outer office, and for a second she didn't even recognize the sound. Then when she did, she poked her head out of the kitchen; still no one was there. It was the line to Devries Construction. She walked to her desk; her hand hesitated over the receiver, and she wondered if she was supposed to continue any of her work. It stopped ringing.

Reminded of her list, she hooked up her work computer to the cables on her desk. She clicked through to the remote server and found the location file for the cameras that she'd set up in the warehouse. She put in the time and date that she'd handed over the keys and watched.

First Platon and Stratigos with his three men went inside and did nothing but look around, nod, and shake hands. They passed out of view of one camera and into another. The wide bay doors at the back of the warehouse started to slide open as a huge ride-on dolly approached. It halted until the doors were open all the way and secured. Whoever was driving knew the protocol of delivering to warehouses. A local worker.

He brought in the delivery and they secured it, leaving it on the transport. She zoomed in, looking for some identifying feature. If she couldn't, she'd have to go back down there herself to see. There was none. No brand name on the plastic covering, no hint what it could be.

The phone clanged again, making her jump. It sounded totally different in the empty, sad office. She picked it up, playing receptionist; it was Platon.

She "picked up" the transferred call. "Inventory Management, how can I help you?"

"*Koukla mou*, how are you?"

"Fine, thank you," she replied with a smile so wide that he was sure to hear it and believe she was happy to hear from him. "Why don't you call me on my cell phone anymore? We never get to speak in private nowadays." She put a pout in her voice.

His voice tightened. "Stratigos took my cell phone with your number in it. He makes me use this phone because he likes to tape-record our calls. In case one of us gets, um, 'unruly,' he calls it."

"Is he listening in now?" She twirled the cord around her finger, wondering where he was going with all this.

"No, *koukla mou*, but I can't speak for long. Can you meet me later? Say, at about four?"

"Of course," she said. "Usual place?"

"Yes. I will see you then. I've missed you." His voice nearly cracked on the last word, before he hung up.

What in the world was going on? She wondered if she could trick him into exposing Stratigos's plan. He didn't sound as if he was working from an entirely stable emotional base, and she could probably leverage that in some way.

While she had the phone in her hand, she called her father. He wasn't usually comforting, but he was family, and she needed to hear a friendly voice. Well, friendly-ish. It was four a.m. in DC, so she called the house. He picked up immediately.

"Walker."

"Dad, it's me," she said, hoping he wouldn't ask, "Who?" as he'd done once or twice before.

"Sadie? To what do I owe this pleasure?" He rustled some papers, and she smiled. Typical that he'd already be working in the house at four a.m.

"I need some advice, I guess. No one's been able to find Director Lassiter—he's in Spain somewhere—but Sebastian Seeker had a heart attack at the office and died last night, and everyone else is out of the country. Mr. Shaw from the State Department shut the office down, and I still have an operation going. Oh, and Simon's here." She sighed. It felt like she should just pack up and go home.

"Sadie," he said. And then he chuckled. And then he laughed out loud.

"Daddy," she admonished.

"I'm sorry, darling, but when you put it like that, it sounds like I unleashed a wrecking ball by putting you there." He cleared his throat and stopped laughing. "What kind of operation?"

She filled him in on her gut feeling about Platon, and meeting Stratigos and how they pulled her into doing favors for them. She didn't really have anything else to say; it sounded a little weak, even to her. Despite everything, she should have at least had an idea about what they were planning.

"Sadie. I put you there for a reason. I knew this wasn't going to be an easy assignment, what with your idiot station chief and the G20 meeting coming up. I'm sorry about Seeker, and I confess I hadn't heard about Shaw, although that doesn't surprise me—State, and Shaw in particular, are always keen to shut us down for one reason or another. And, in the interests of full disclosure, Simon called me a couple of days ago, expressing concern that you were involved in something bad." He snorted gently. "Of course, I couldn't tell him that was precisely why you were there."

"You knew Director Lassiter was useless?" Layers of tension seemed to disappear now that she'd confided in him.

"Of course. I wasn't overjoyed at your acceptance into the field, but your test scores and appraisals were excellent. I had faith that you'd bloom wherever I sent you. But if I had sent you to a different city, where the local station chief was stellar, where there was little risk, and where the operation ran like a finely tuned mechanism, you would have stagnated for three years. You might not have realized it, but that kind of first assignment is difficult to climb out of if you want a career out there, away from Langley."

His words put her four months into perspective in an instant. She wasn't making a rookie mistake with Platon; she *was* on to something. This wasn't the "soft" assignment her fellow trainees at The Farm had claimed. Her back straightened and her shoulders lost their tension like a dam being washed away.

"Thank you, Dad. I guess I better un-break into the office before anyone from the embassy finds me."

"That's the spirit. I trust you to get this done. How many days until the president lands?"

She looked at the whiteboard that she'd last updated the day before. "Fifteen now."

"Good, then I expect an update from you, soon. Use every resource you have at your disposal. That's the key to being a good operative." He was silent for a moment. "You're doing well, Sadie. I suspect I haven't said that too often to you. But I'm proud of you."

Unshed tears prickled behind her eyes. She was about to thank him, but he'd hung up. Which in itself was typical emotion avoidance from him. She looked at her watch, with a new sense of urgency and direction.

She had plenty of time to get back to the port and check the contents of the delivery Stratigos had put in the warehouse, and get back to shower before meeting Platon.

CHAPTER TWENTY

Simon was staking out Sadie's apartment, splitting his attention between the photos that Garrett had sent him and the entrance to her building. He'd considered just waiting inside, but he didn't want to start this meeting with another argument, and from the tracker in her bag, he knew she was making her way back home.

Dammit—just when he'd been ready to reconcile, his mission had basically wrapped itself around her. Maybe the universe was telling him to back off. To pull the plug on this relationship and her and to move the fuck on. He couldn't afford to be blindsided by something because she was taking up so much of his concentration. Women fucked up the mission. They always did.

By the time he caught sight of her, it was nearly two in the afternoon. He was jumped up on the coffee he'd been mainlining in the café across from her apartment, and he'd totally convinced himself that getting involved with Sadie again was the worst idea.

Seeing her hustle up the steps did nothing to quell any of his feelings. She looked as if she was in a rush, had something to do. But what could she be in a hurry for with her office closed and nothing to do until her coworker's funeral? He wanted to shake her. What was she involved in?

He strode up to her door and knocked maybe more aggressively than the situation called for. She opened the door without looking.

"Simon! What are you—?"

He went in without being asked to. "Don't answer the door without looking to see who it is," he demanded, realizing immediately that he'd gone off track before he'd even established a track to take.

She closed the door behind him with a puzzled look on her face. "There is no peephole. There rarely is in Europe. So I either open it without looking, or I never open my door. And if I did the latter, you would not be in here with that accusatory look on your face. Which I'm beginning to wish was the case."

Suddenly he wished he had actual photos that he could throw on the bed and order her to look at. But those were the old days. Today he had to show her the photos on his phone, hoping the screen wouldn't go dark before he'd get a read on her expression.

"I have something I need you to look at," he said, sitting awkwardly on the bed and putting in the password to his phone.

She remained standing, a quizzical look on her face. "Seriously? I'm in kind of a hurry. This couldn't wait until tonight? You said you wanted to talk then."

"This couldn't wait." He patted the bed with even more awkwardness. Damn—he was supposed to be in charge here and he was patting the bed like he was a teenager trying to persuade a girl to sit next to him. This wasn't going quite how he wanted it to. He needed to treat her like any suspect, not his ex.

"We need to talk now. So sit your ass down and look at these photos."

She shot him a slightly amused look that tilted her lips in a way that shouldn't have been as distracting as it was. "Look." He thrust the phone under her chin and swiped through the photos, careful to stop before she saw any of his personal ones. She pulled the phone down, away from her eyes a little, and watched again as he scrolled backward.

"I'm not sure who that is," she said, pointing at Stamov. "I've never seen him before."

"He's the Russian finance minister. Anatov Stamov."

A wave of recognition passed over her face before she buttoned her expression back down into nothing more than interest. But he'd seen it—he was sure. "Tell me what you know."

"I've heard of him, but I'm not sure I've ever seen him," she said slowly.

Immediately, he knew what was happening. She was speaking slowly to give herself time to formulate an answer. At that sign, his heart plummeted. The part of him that wanted her so badly, who still loved her, fractured and fled his body.

"Do you know what he was doing with your boyfriend's 'uncle'?" He used douchey air quotes because he couldn't help himself. He was furious with himself. He'd fallen for her, hook, line, and sinker, and now he wondered if that was always her plan. Always. Playing damsel in distress in Mumbai, trying to seduce him that first night. Maybe her daddy issues went so deep that she'd defected to another side. Maybe even the Russians. Goddamnit. He didn't have time for this.

"So you have no idea why your friend, the terrorist, would be meeting a Russian minister?" he asked with, he hoped, deceptive mildness.

"Well, when you put it like that, it does sound kind of bad. I'm about to go see his nephew, actually, so I can ask him about it if you like."

He forced his lips into a smile and leaned in to nuzzle her neck. "I'd appreciate that." He kissed her jawline and was gratified to hear her almost purr. Gratified and aroused. *Keep it together, Tennant.*

She turned and kissed him as naturally as if they had been together for years, and he lost himself in it. Remembered their relationship, their love, the feeling of peace he'd only ever had with her.

And then he handcuffed her to the bed with a wire cable tie.

"What the—?" she said in surprise. "I can't reach you from here." And then her expression changed. "Oh. This isn't for sex, then?" A flush reached her cheeks as if she was embarrassed, and he felt a twinge of guilt.

"Not for sex. I'll be back here in a few hours to debrief you, before I turn you over to your father. He hoped he sounded more certain than he felt. Judging by her expression, he'd convinced her.

"You bastard! As soon as I get out of these, I'm going to call the police and have you arrested for lying, cheating, and being a foreign operative on their sovereign soil." She crossed her legs and tipped her chin up. "You better hope I don't get to you before the police do."

"You don't scare me, sweetheart. Not even a little."

"And that only serves to show your stupidity. I feel sorry for you, really."

"Well, thank you for your sympathy, Sadie. I can't wait to see your father explain to Congress what his daughter was doing, cavorting with terrorists."

She narrowed her eyes. "I've never cavorted in my life. And I pity you even more if you bring my father into this. I'll even visit you in prison." She clamped her mouth shut.

His temper was getting the best of him. Sadie and he had never argued, not once, and for the love of God it felt great to shout at her. To finally stop avoiding their real feelings. "Your father isn't that powerful, Sadie. I don't know what the Intelligence Committee would do if asked to choose between my boss, a very well-decorated, career military man, or a politician like your father, who has a terrorist for a daughter. Hmm. Let me think about that." His voice lowered but gained in intensity. "They would fire your father's ass and give my boss another medal. So you are shit out of luck, sweetheart. You can sit there and be thankful I didn't wait until you were naked before securing you. Think about what you've done." He opened the door and slammed it after him. Just the thought of her naked and handcuffed made his jeans tighten.

She's a traitor, dammit. Get your mind out of your pants.

* * *

Sadie cursed at Simon as he left. She didn't give him the satisfaction of saying the words out loud, or yelling, or fighting, or screaming. She just wanted to kick him in the nuts and watch as he writhed in pain. She gave herself a moment to visualize that, and it calmed her as she knew it would.

But then she shrugged. He knew she was some kind of operative, and aside from the fact that he hurdled all sense and jumped to the conclusion that she was an enemy, he still left her only handcuffed with zip ties, which weren't impossible to get out of. Difficult, but not impossible.

Damn Simon. She looked at her bedside clock and saw she was already late to meet Platon. She lay back on the bed and tried to reach her go bag with her foot. She couldn't, but thankfully the bed frame wasn't attached to the floor. She dragged the bed, inch by painful inch, to where she could hook her foot around the strap of the bag and pull it to her.

Exhausted, she flopped back on the bed for a couple of seconds, her wrists aching from the pressure of pulling the bed with the restraints attached. After a few deep breaths, she jerked the bag up on top of the bed and emptied it with her feet. The last thing out was her key chain. In actuality, it was less of a key chain and more of a multitool. Corkscrew, bottle opener, thumb-pressure lights in green and red that could be used for Morse code messages, detachable chem lights, and a Swiss Army knife. Not one of those touristy ones with the scissors and nail file, but a hard-core sharp one. She moved it toward her hand so she could grab it and open it with her teeth. Then came the hard part.

Angling it downward toward her wrists, she could only make a small sawing motion with it. And every time she pressed down, the tip of the knife slid against her skin, making a graze at first and then a full-blown cut. A rivulet of blood was trickling down her arm.

Her fingers started cramping, and stretching them out lost the knife to the floor. She picked it up with her feet and started over. She looked at the clock again. She'd been working at this for an hour. She'd have to call Platon as soon as possible to let him know she was running late.

Except...*shit*. He'd taken her phone. It was only a burner phone, but still. Just one more thing to kick him in the junk for. Or something.

She went back to her knife. Her thumb and wrist sharply cramped as she sawed over and over. Not wanting to risk losing the knife again, she tried to push through the pain, mind over matter. In her mind she was in the temple to Poseidon that stood on a high cliff just a short bus ride away from Athens. As the waves folded in on the beach, then straightened and pulled back to the sea, she breathed in time with them and pressed with the knife, down for every wave. A small part of her brain registered the sting of the blade on her wrist, but with closed eyes she moved her brain past the pain and out to the sea.

She was deep into her visualization when her wrists suddenly moved. Her eyes flew open and saw that a full half of the tie had been cut. Carefully, she put the knife on the bed, maneuvered her feet so they were against the footboard where her hands were tied, and pulled her hands back and apart, yanking them with all her upper-body strength.

The ties snapped with a satisfying crack, leaving the outsides of her wrists as achy as the insides were cut. A flood of satisfaction rushed through her as she ran to the bathroom to run her hands and wrists under the cold faucet. It felt heavenly after the pressure and pain that had wrought hell on them.

Checking the clock again, she wondered if it was even worth going to find Platon. Except she really wanted to see if he would confide any more information about Stratigos's plans—assuming he even knew them. She slipped Band-Aids onto her cuts, pulled on a long-sleeved blouse, despite the heat, and turned back to the room. If Simon returned, she wanted it to look as if nothing had happened. She disposed of the remaining parts of the wrist ties, pulled the bed back to where it had been, and repacked her go bag into a different, slightly larger purse so there would be no evidence left in the apartment.

She stopped in her tracks for a moment and looked around the room. Was this how her life would always be? Hiding things from the people she cared about? Paranoid that she'd leave the wrong phone on the counter, that she'd have to explain an injury. She rubbed her wrist and paused. This was something she'd have to think about when all this was over. She'd chosen this life, and she'd recited an oath when she passed out of The Farm. So for now, she had a job to do.

* * *

The café where she'd agreed to meet Platon was busy, and for a minute she thought he'd already left. But on pushing farther inside, she found him with a half-empty drink in front of him, slumped against the wall with his eyes closed.

"Platon! Are you all right?" She took the seat next to him and pulled on his arm.

He roused and smiled. "You came, *koukla mou*. I thought you'd forgotten me." He pressed his fist in front of his mouth, and for a second she thought he was going to throw up. But instead he suppressed a loud burp and then laughed. "Excuse me." Except it came out as "essuzeme."

Great. Now she wasn't going to get anything useful from him. "Do you want me to get you a taxi to take you home?" she asked, preparing to stand and look for a waiter.

"Noooo. I can't go home." He put his finger in front of his mouth. "They're watching my apartment. Shhhhh." He giggled and then drooped against the wall again.

Sadie was conflicted. She should ask the waiter for a coffee and water for him, but was there any other chance she could get more information from him first before he sobered up?

"What did you put in my warehouse, sweetie? Can you tell me?" She stroked his back in what she hoped was a comforting way.

"The C-4? I can't tell you about it. It's a secret. Shhhhhh," he said again.

Her blood ran cold. If that's what that huge delivery was, it was enough C-4 to level an entire city block. Perhaps more. She pictured it piled high on the motorized dolly. Definitely more. Sweet Jesus, what were they planning on blowing up?

She adopted a scolding tone. "Platon, what in the world did Stratigos get you involved in?"

His head snapped up. And then he started laughing hysterically. People nearby started looking at them, and Sadie didn't need the scrutiny.

"Shh. Platon. You must keep your voice down."

"Shhhhhhh," he repeated, and then giggled. "Don't tell the Russians."

Platon was clearly the worst person in the world to share a secret with.

"What can't we tell the Russians, sweetie?" She had to push this as far as she could.

"Stratigos hates them, but they have lots of money. They give him lots of money. I saw it. I got some!" Seriously, he was like a fourteen-year-old boy when he was drunk.

"How much did you get?" she asked, smiling at him encouragingly.

"Three thousand euros for the keys to the warehouse. Another ten thousand to drive some people around." He just looked sleepy now.

"That's so cool. Where are you driving people to?" she asked.

"Away from the embassy before it goes boom." He made an explosion noise and gestured a ka-boom with his hands.

Her heart stuttered. "The American embassy?" she asked in horror. This was really not what she was expecting to hear.

"Pffft. No. The Russian embassy, not the 'merican one." He hiccupped. "No, but they'll be blamed. He said it was a good plan. A big enough distraction." He was frowning now, as if he didn't quite believe it. "I feel sick, *koukla mou*. I should go home."

"I thought you said you didn't want to go home?" she said, gesturing for a waiter.

"I don't remember. Did I? This is bad, isn't it? I'm a bad person." He tried to get up but couldn't balance between the chair and the table, and sat back down heavily.

"Is there someone outside of the city you can stay with tonight?"

He nodded. "S'good ideas. Okay."

The waiter arrived and helped him out of the café and into a taxi. When he came back, she asked him how much Platon owed him, and paid his tab. Her head was reeling. They were plotting with the Russians to blow up the Russian embassy? That was the most bizarre thing she'd ever heard. But then Simon had shown her photos of Stratigos and the Russian finance minister looking thick as thieves. He had to be right. And it was a distraction? A big enough distraction for what? If leveling the whole embassy was just the distraction, how huge was the real thing going to be?

CHAPTER TWENTY-ONE

Simon and Garrett were sitting in a rental car outside the warehouse.

"This is it, mate," Garrett said. "The holy grail has to be in here. Sadie's linked here, her boyfriend, the boyfriend's uncle-slash-known terrorist. It all leads to here."

Simon nodded and checked his phone. His tracker said Sadie was still in her apartment. He still had no idea what to do with her. Let her go? Turn her over to the authorities? Maybe the only good option *was* to call her father to come get her and let him decide what to do with her. Yes. That's what he would do. Assuming Walker took his call.

"Tennant?" Garrett said. "You're miles away. Are you ready to go?"

"Yup." He reached for the door handle just as Garrett put his hand up to stop him. "Wait," he whispered.

They both froze. The motion-detector light in front of the warehouse came on as six or seven men approached the door.

Simon and Garrett scooched down in their seats and tried to watch. Dusk was making the shadows blue and the sky gray, but still they could see that one of the men was Stratigos.

As the last man entered and the door swung shut behind them, Simon and Garrett jumped out of the car and chambered a round in their guns. As they were crossing to the door, there was some shouting and a shot from inside the warehouse. The men looked at each other and skirted the side of the building. On one side there was a small staircase with a wooden handrail that led to an office where the floor manager could keep his eyes on everything.

They took the steps, pausing to listen with each one. Simon tried the door. It was locked, of course. He took a knife out of his back pocket and slid it between the door and the frame where the handle was. The wood cracked inward just enough to pull the door free. He opened it a fraction to see if anyone had heard the noise of the wood splintering. Nope. It seemed as if they were arguing down in the warehouse. He turned to Garrett and shrugged.

Garrett just smiled and nodded. Simon wondered if anything in the world could faze him.

They crept across a walkway to the office and went in, closing the door softly behind them. And then Simon saw something that couldn't have fazed himself more.

Sadie.

How the hell was she loose? He sat with his back against the office wall and checked his app again. Yup—it was still showing that she was in her apartment. Damn her. Now there was no pretending she wasn't involved; she'd have to appear in his report. Except, something was niggling at a corner of his brain. Something she'd said in her apartment. What had it been? The nugget of something remained just out of reach. *Damn.*

He took a breath and tamped down all the other feelings and thoughts that coursed around. The fact that they could never be together now. That he wouldn't be growing old with her or be able to see their children grow up. Children who already had names.

Suddenly numbness came, and he realized that he hadn't felt mission-numb since before Mumbai, when he met Sadie. Before her, he was able to switch off everything and be the soldier machine he'd been trained to be. Calculating, mission focused. While he was with her, there was always a chink in his armor. Always a way to escape the mission in memories. He had nothing now.

Except his need to have this mission *over.*

* * *

Sadie had gone to the warehouse to see how easy it might be to get rid of the C-4 explosives. All the way there she was plotting different disposal methods. She hadn't come up with a whole lot. She could call her father, but she didn't want to unless she had no other options. Calling Daddy for help wouldn't win her any points with anyone, and certainly no one in the State Department was going to help.

The port was deserted, so she was able to just walk in. The guard knew her. They all did. Even though the warehouse looked empty, the knowledge of what was inside grated her nerves into shreds. She let herself into the building and, back against the door, rifled in her bag for some items that she then stashed in her belt and pockets.

There were huge overhead lights, but she didn't want to switch them on. The upper part of the building had a small row of windows at the top that looked out over one part of the harbor, and she didn't want to advertise to anyone that she was there by making the place look like a lighthouse.

With her penlight, she ascertained that all the fake construction materials were all still there and in the condition they'd been left in. There was a chance that Stratigos and Platon hadn't discovered that this warehouse wasn't what it seemed.

The pallets of C-4 hadn't moved. They loomed ominously in the center of the room, easily measuring about eight feet by five feet around and maybe seven feet tall, although with the height of the dolly, the cargo was maybe nine feet high. If she could only remember the usual brick size of C-4, she was sure there was some amazing equation that she'd probably never be able to do that would tell her how many bricks there were. She was going to have to look.

With her penlight in her mouth, she carefully slit the plastic covering near the bottom at the corner—a slit that might look accidental, as if it had gotten caught on something. She eased the tightly wrapped sheeting up as far as she could.

Her brain numbed when she saw the mass of bricks. There were easily five hundred or so. And those were just the ones she could count. She looked for the mark on them. Stamped at the end was a US code. Langley could tell her where they came from, but for now it was just bad enough that they were man-ufactured in the US. She was beginning to understand how deep the desire was to blame whatever they had planned on the Americans. Right down to the origin of the explosives. All they'd wanted from her was the warehouse.

Sadie sat back on her heels for a moment and just stared at the cream-colored blocks, looking for anything like benign pottery clay, waiting to be made into something beautiful. A light sweat erupted on her forehead. She was out of her depth here. Why hadn't she told Simon? He'd know exactly what to do.

You couldn't tell him because that would be breaking the law.

She knew that was true, but she couldn't help thinking that there must be legitimate times when it couldn't be helped. Even as the thought trickled across her mind, she knew there wasn't. Because if she told someone, it wasn't just her she would be outing, but the people she worked with, the entire entity of Devries Construction. It was just too dangerous. Not to mention dangerous to the person she'd have told.

She stood. Okay. There was no real dispute that this was go-ing to be used for something really bad. And that she—

A light appeared from somewhere. She peeked around the pallet and saw that the outside motion-sensor light had flicked on outside the door. *Shit. Shit.*

She took a breath. Maybe it was a cat walking by. Rats, maybe. The sound of the key sliding into the lock echoed around the room.

Well, definitely one kind of rat. Sadie switched off her pen-light and looked for somewhere to hide. She opted for the excavator—mainly because it had so many parts jutting out of it; it would be easy to conceal herself in its shadows without drawing attention.

And then the whole warehouse flooded with light, just as she darted behind the driver's cabin. She hoped this was just a look-see visit, a show-and-tell, because if they tried to take that C-4 anywhere, she was going to have to step in and stop them. And God knew she had no idea how to do that.

There seemed to be a bunch of men, judging by the echoing voices, maybe six or seven. She wished the echo weren't distorting their words so much; from where she was, they could just as well be discussing the weather. She inched as close to them as she dared.

From the vantage point of just behind the bucket part of the digger, she could see Stratigos and five other men. The old man slapped the C-4 several times, like he might the rump of a winning racehorse. Pride had puffed up his chest. He was trying to impress these men. And they were speaking English—she caught the odd word or two, but nothing that made sense.

So the other men were obviously not Greek. She just hoped they weren't American. The Glock her brother had given her was nestled in the small of her back, under her black shirt. She knew better than to reach for it, though. She was hoping they'd just leave, but when she caught Stratigos looking at his watch a couple of times, she realized they were waiting for someone.

A click echoed around the warehouse, and something metallic pressed against the back of her head. Her stomach dropped and her heart raced. Was this it? She showed her hands immediately and took a second to figure out what attitude to take. All she'd done was hide.

"What do you think you're doing?" she said loudly and in an aggravated voice.

The voices stopped and several other guns were cocked. Great. Let's hope she could pull it off.

"Who is it?" Stratigos spat out.

"Platon's girl." The man with the gun to her head pushed her toward the men.

"How *dare* you? Put that away. This isn't the Wild West, you know," she said.

"And you would know, being American. Strange to find one who is scared of a gun," Stratigos said with a smile that didn't translate into anything reassuring. He'd been trying to impress the other men before, was showing the C-4 off like it was his own personal creation. Maybe she needed to change tack.

"Canadian. I'm Canadian," she said. "I'm so sorry to bust in on you like that, sir. I'd forgotten something in the office this week, and I wanted to come get it. But before I could get up there, you came in and I was scared. So I hid. If you don't mind, I can just go get my day planner and be out of here."

He paused and regarded her for a moment. For that solitary moment, she thought she'd nailed it.

"No," he said with finality. He nodded to the man with the gun behind her, who pushed her to her knees.

"This is the perfect way to assure that we are all in this together," he said slowly to the other men. "There is no backing out. No reneging. Are we in accord, comrades?"

Fuck. He didn't even care if she was telling the truth or not.

She'd been so sure that he was just a string puller—an old anarchist planning to disrupt the G20 talks. Even when Platon told her about the C-4, she'd only concentrated on the explosives and not the man with the willingness to use them. Rookie. *Rookie.*

She'd been so intent on proving herself to her father, the trainers at The Farm, her loser boss, and even Sebastian that she'd ignored the signs. She hadn't shifted her opinions as the facts had changed. A lesson learned. Except now she'd had no time to learn from it. Simon had been right about Stratigos. A simple terrorist.

Simon. How could she just die, or more likely—as far as he would be concerned—just disappear, leaving him thinking she was a traitor? He'd never know that she was shielding him from the truth. He'd live out his life thinking her love for him had been a lie. He'd move on, try to erase her from his mind. She'd just disappear.

The men nodded at what Stratigos said. He pointed at each one, insisting they spoke.

"Da."

"Da."

"Da."

Nyet. She wasn't going to stick around for the other yeses. No way. She *was* going to see Simon again. She was going to get out of this or die trying. She placed both hands on the floor in front of her and kicked up one leg, making contact with the gunman's knee. He grunted in pain as something in his kneecap snapped audibly. His gun went off as he staggered backward, but the bullet ricocheted off the floor and made the other men jump away and take cover.

She rolled under the excavator and popped up on the other side, reaching for her gun. She pulled the slide back to chamber a round. Bullets pinged off the digger, one perilously close to her ear. She crouched behind the huge wheel and pondered her options. One down, six to go.

The gunfire stopped when they realized that shooting at a huge metal vehicle wasn't a successful strategy. She heard someone barking orders. If they came around the digger from both sides, she was done for.

Of course, that was exactly what they did. She tried to steady her breathing as she contemplated running. But there was nowhere to run to. Damn the CIA for not equipping the warehouse with more things she could hide behind.

Her mind racing on pure adrenaline, she crouched and looked at the floor directly ahead of her. She'd just have to watch for the first man to breach the corner of the vehicle in her peripheral vision and then take a shot. It was the only way she even had a chance.

A shot rang out in the silence, and then another. Two different guns. Who the hell were they shooting at if it wasn't her?

CHAPTER TWENTY-TWO

When Simon had seen Sadie on her knees with a gun at her head, he'd realized what he should have seen much, much earlier: she was not on the terrorists' side. As he'd set his laser on the back of the man's head, he remembered what had been eluding him—he'd threatened to blow her cover and she'd said that she'd see him in prison. It was illegal to reveal a covert operative's identity, punishable by imprisonment. She was still CIA.

As if to reiterate what a completely blind fool he'd been, the men standing in front of Sadie were all saying yes in Russian. Yes, he was a fucking idiot. Yes, he had allowed his personal feelings of betrayal to seep into his professional life. Yes, he'd have to grovel for forgiveness.

He flexed his trigger finger, about to take the shot before all the yes men had finished agreeing to kill her, when the man dropped out of sight. He pulled his eye away from the gunsight and saw that she'd disabled the man and rolled under the excavator.

A flood of pride rushed through him. Pride that absolutely wasn't his place to feel.

"Garrett," he whispered.

"I saw that. You think she's a company girl?"

He didn't hesitate. "Yes." He didn't know for sure, but he was choosing to trust and believe in her. That was all. For the first time in his life, he was willing to risk everything to trust one person. It was everything he'd been trained not to do. And it felt righteous.

"Well, let's go get her six," Garrett said, double-checking his magazine again.

"Thanks, man," Simon said. He actually had zero doubt that he could take out seven guys by himself. Zero doubt. Garrett didn't have to follow him into the line of fire.

"Don't get mushy on me, mate."

He took the stairs, his weapon up to his eye. He spotted one Russian, who shot wildly at the stairs. Simon exhaled, taking his shot calmly, and dropped him by the pallet in the middle of the floor. He spun back toward the digger, where Sadie had been seconds ago. She was nowhere to be seen, and neither were the guys he'd seen approaching her.

He swung back, as Garrett flanked him, sweeping the area in the opposite direction. They headed to the racks of smaller supplies on the other side of the warehouse. As they made their way down separate aisles, Simon's phone went off. He muffled a curse.

Garrett piped up from the next aisle. "Thank you for calling. I'm sorry I can't get to the phone right now, as I need both hands to maim and destroy. Please leave a message—" A grunt, followed by an expletive and a snapping sound, broke into his monologue.

Simon stopped and shoved a box through the shelf so he could see what was happening. He couldn't see anything. Then Garrett popped up from the floor.

He placed a semiautomatic machine gun in the space on the shelf that Simon had cleared, and said, "One down."

Simon nodded to the weapon. "You don't want that?"

"I'm better with a short and my hands. I thought I should give you dibs on it since this is your clusterf— I mean, op." Garrett's shit-eating grin was really starting to get on his nerves.

"You know when you smile like that, I just want to punch my fist through your head, right?" he growled.

"That's what I count on. People who hate me are predictable in their actions. People who love me aren't. Words to live by, my friend," he said.

"Dick," Simon said. As he turned back in the direction he'd been sweeping the aisle, something fell on him from above.

He smashed against the metal shelving, disoriented. It wasn't something; it was someone. He crouched down and ran at his assailant, slamming him into the other side of the aisle with a bone-jarring force that did nothing for his already jarred brain.

The man appeared to have no reaction to being rammed against the hard metal fixtures. He pounded his fists against Simon's neck and shoulders, making him slump to the floor, only just spinning out of the way of a kick to the head. His gun had skittered away under the shelving when the man had dropped on him.

He shook his head, trying to clear it. Objects were being poked out of the shelving, and he assumed it was Garrett trying to get a shot. But judging by the fallen boxes, he was at least three meters ahead of them.

With a roar, the Russian charged at him. Simon crouched at the last minute and, grabbing the man's jacket, used his momentum to throw him over his back. The man fell to the floor but jumped up in a matter of seconds. This guy was like the fucking Terminator.

Instead of waiting for the man to make his move, Simon took the fight to him. He ran at him and executed a move he'd only successfully done once. He achieved full speed as he grabbed the front of the man's clothes and slid between his legs, yanking him headfirst to the floor. The crack echoed around the warehouse.

Simon slumped, bracing his hands on his knees, and took a breath. His body was getting too old for this shit.

"You okay?" Garrett said from the other aisle.

"Yup," he replied shortly, not wanting to say much more that would betray his panting. He turned and straightened. He couldn't believe his eyes.

The Russian man was getting to his feet, blood pouring down his face. He dipped his head as if he were about to run at Simon again.

"Uh, you know when I said I was all right?" he said to Garrett.

There was a gunshot. The Russian's stomach exploded in front of Simon's eyes, but his feet kept moving. He took one, two, three paces before dropping to his knees.

Standing behind him was Sadie, gun raised. He smiled.

She pointed her fingers at her eyes and then poked them toward the pallet in the middle of the floor. He nodded, trying to stop smiling. She bent down and fished his gun out from under the shelving, kicking it toward him. He held up his finger and approached her, picking up his weapon as he went. He looked around the end of the shelving and then turned back to her. Without saying a word, he planted a kiss on her surprised lips. Firm, hard, an "I'm not going anywhere" kiss.

There was another volley of shots, and Simon caught a man crouching behind the pallet. He rested his arm on Sadie's shoulder and waited for him to poke his head out. It took only two seconds for Simon to shoot him in his arm. The man screamed and slumped against the cargo they'd watched be delivered earlier that week.

Garrett appeared beside them. "I think that's them all except one. Our terrorist friend did a runner as soon as we started shooting back. I imagine he's halfway back to Athens by now. But don't worry. I can get my police friend to pick him up, and whoever's left here."

"I'm Sadie," she said, holding her hand out to Garrett.

He didn't give her his name. "I know who you are. You're the one who's been fucking with my friend here's head."

Simon looked down at her, relief taking the edge off his words. "He's lying. We're not friends."

She laughed. And then paused, a frown passing over her face.

"What is it?"

"The top of the C-4 is flashing."

"What? What C-4? That's C-4?" Garrett pointed at the cargo. "Holy fucking shit, man." He walked around the pallet slowly. "It's definitely flashing something."

They all looked up at the red flashing light. "I guess you better give me a bunk up," Garrett said.

"A what?" Simon and Sadie said in concert.

Garrett rolled his eyes. "An assist. I'm going up there to see what's flashing."

Simon put his hands together so that Garrett could step in them. When he did, he hefted him upward so he could climb on top.

"Bollocks," he said. "Have any of you done any bomb disposal?"

"What? No. It can't be rigged. It was just bricks of C-4. Inert," Sadie said, glancing in horror at Simon.

"Well, someone rigged it while we were otherwise occupied. Jesus. Every time I do any work with you Yanks, there are explosives involved. I do not like explosives. So...who's done any defusing?"

Garrett peered down from the top of the C-4.

"Ah, I did a webinar?" Sadie stammered.

"A webinar?" Garrett said. "Is that how you're trained nowadays? God help us."

"It sounds like more training than you've had," Sadie retorted with her hands on her hips, gun still in her hand.

Simon wished he could take a photo. She looked so cute. And then pondered the tongue-lashing he'd get if she knew that he thought she looked cute.

"Help me up," he said to Garrett.

Garrett dangled down a hand and Simon caught it and climbed up the side. He could see immediately that they weren't going to defuse it. He said as much to Garrett in a low voice.

"What? What did you say?" Sadie shouted.

There were four minutes on the clock and a motion-sensor trip wire. There was no way he could defuse it in four minutes. He eyed the cargo door and then sighed.

"Okay, let's go."

"What are you doing?" Sadie said. "We have to defuse it. It can't blow. This building is owned by the US government, and the C-4 is US manufactured. If it blows, it will look like we were planning something hideous. And that seems to be what the Russians want. We can't leave it here."

There were so many questions he had for her and zero time. His mind filtered the important information and locked away the rest. He had one option.

He turned to Garrett. "Get her out of here, and get far away. Plausible-deniability far away."

Garrett, for his part, didn't hesitate. He climbed down, grabbed her arm, and pulled her toward the door.

"No, wait!" Sadie protested.

"No," Simon said. "We have a lot to talk about. Afterward. This is my job. Trust me, and go."

She stared at him a second and then nodded, letting Garrett pull her toward the door.

As soon as it was closed, he ran to the other side of the warehouse and pressed the large red button to open the big cargo doors. He had three minutes. He looked for the wires on the motorized dolly and pulled them free to hot-wire the engine.

Two minutes.

He jumped on the dolly and floored the accelerator. Of course it asthmatically turned and chugged as fast as a golf cart towing a few tons of golf clubs, which is to say, not fast.

Thirty seconds.

The waft of air from the doors cooled his sweat-soaked brow. His heart picked up. He wasn't going to make it. There wasn't enough time to reach the water. It was over.

* * *

The British guy dragged her to the car, pushed her in, and ran around to the driver's seat. He pumped the gas and squealed out of their parking place, leaving rubber on the road.

She was trying to keep track of the seconds ticking down. Where was Simon? How was he going to survive? She twisted around in the car seat to look out of the rear window.

"He'll be all right, won't he?" she asked, knowing he couldn't possibly know.

"We'll know soon," he said, eyes flicking between the road and the rearview mirror.

"Okay. Stop. Stop the car." She'd been stupid to get in the car in the first place, but her brain just hadn't computed what was happening. "Stop. Stop or I'll fucking jump." She opened the car door.

He slammed on the brake. "Keep your knickers on." The car came to an approximate stop and she jumped out.

Simon. Simon. Simon. She chanted his name in time with her steps as she ran back toward the warehouse.

Suddenly a boom reached her, knocking her sideways into the side of another warehouse. The pain staggered her brain as she tried to get up. A jagged piece of metal was stuck in her shoulder. Stuck hard. She channeled what she wanted to scream into a roar as she got to her feet. She looked quickly at the wound, not wanting to dwell on what it actually looked like. The shard was sticking out about five inches. She had no idea how long it was. She started sweating bullets with the pain.

Holding her arm, she ran toward the warehouse. A forklift had been knocked to its side, and car alarms were going off. Someone ran past her shouting, "Earthquake!" in a muffled voice. She didn't think so.

She tried to open the door but the blast seemed to have crumpled the doorframe. On total automatic pilot, she ran around the warehouse. But the building seemed to have grown—it was so much bigger than before. It took so long to get around. It felt as if she were running through molasses. She gritted her teeth just to stay on her feet. Tears swept down her face as she tried to get to him. *Simon. Simon.* Why couldn't she move faster? Where was he? He couldn't have left her. Not without giving her a chance to explain. She hadn't told him that she loved him. Hadn't told him anything. As the pain dug deeper and dragged her down, slowing her more and more until she couldn't go any farther, she rounded the corner facing the harbor and crumpled, sliding down the corrugated siding of the warehouse. Sirens played on the breeze from the opposite side of the harbor.

"Simon," she croaked. She thought she croaked. Her voice was either gone or her hearing had been damaged by the blast. "Simon."

Struggling to keep her eyes open, she tried to see any evidence of the blast. Any evidence that Simon had been there at all. There was nothing to be seen except that the wooden top to the harbor bulkhead had cracked where the hand was.

The hand? She tried to focus. It moved. Someone was in the water. A second hand emerged. She tried to get up, but she couldn't—her legs wouldn't support her. Tucking the hand of her damaged shoulder in her shirt to support it, she crawled on her knees and one hand. Crying. She fell, sprawling on the concrete, but got up and struggled toward the hands. She prayed it was Simon. "Simon. Simon. Simon," she said, having no idea if her voice was working.

A head poked up. It *was* Simon. She cried out in relief and crawled faster. He propped his head on his hands, eyes closed. Breathing hard. He was breathing.

She fell face-first on the ground in her haste to get to him. She took one of his hands in her good hand, stretching across the quay to reach him.

He hauled himself up, moving as if he was as damaged as she was. He flung one leg out and levered himself onto dry land, groaning as he did. He lay next to her, holding her hand.

When they eventually stopped panting with exertion, he said, "That was stupid."

"What? Coming back for you?"

"Leaving without telling me you love me. Okay, *and* coming back for me," he said, obviously in pain.

"I promise. It won't happen again," she groaned, and then, not able to hold her shoulder off the ground anymore, she flopped it down. The jagged pain sent waves of nausea through her and blackness into her eyes. She closed them to try to bat back her roiling stomach, and they stayed closed.

EPILOGUE

Sadie lay on Simon's sofa in his North Carolina home breathing deeply. She'd given up pacing and checking to see if she'd missed a call or a text. She was trying a Zen approach.

Her arm was still in a sling, but she had to go a full two weeks without pain medication to get back on active-duty status, which was back to Athens, back to Devries Construction, and back to Director Lassiter, who had been eventually found with his mistress. No wonder he was unreachable at the golf resorts they'd tried. He'd been brought back to Langley for some "remedial counseling" and was due to retake his position as station chief in Athens two weeks after she returned.

The British guy, whom she now knew as Malone Garrett, had found them and made sure it was the embassy ambulance that came to get them. That way they could hide that they'd even been there. Malone had then disappeared into the ether, after racking up an obscene room service bill. Simon had just laughed.

They still didn't know what the Russians were trying to distract everyone from, but they had a whole new cadre of operatives working their contacts. The Russian finance minister was recalled to Russia and had disappeared. Had he failed in his mission? No one knew that or even what his mission to distract was all about. Nevertheless, all US agencies were on high alert.

Simon had sustained internal bruising in the blast. The dolly hadn't moved fast enough for him to jump off before it hit the water, so he had to stay on, only jumping clear when it was actually over the bulkhead. He'd just been pulling himself out when the charges blew, slamming him against the harbor wall. It was a miracle he'd survived. A real, God's honest miracle. No doctor could believe he virtually walked away from the underwater shock wave.

It was a miracle that they'd decided they weren't going to waste.

She looked up at the sound of a car squealing to a halt outside the house and hauled herself up, trying not to rumple her white silk dress and silk sling.

He burst through the door in a suit, carrying a bouquet of flowers. When he saw her, he stopped and placed a hand on his heart. Then he held up his finger, dragged out his phone, and took a photo. "I just want to always remember you like this. Beautiful, rolling your eyes, and suffering from a battle injury. You're perfect."

Her heart filled up. He'd been so much freer with her this time, been so much more open, more lighthearted. She didn't know why—maybe because they now understood what they each did at work. Maybe they trusted each other more. Maybe they were just in love. Horribly, cringeworthily in love.

"Come over here and say that, mister," she said.

Clearly he didn't need to be asked twice. He ditched the flowers on the sofa and swung her up in his arms.

She laughed as he carefully deposited her on their bed, being sure not to move her arm too much.

He stood and frowned. "We need to get that dress off you."

With her sling and shoulder injury, she knew it would take too long. "You know, maybe it needs some rumples in it. After all, it won't do to look too fancy now, will it?" Their elopement was planned carefully to be the antithesis of their original wedding plans.

Simon didn't need persuading. He shucked off all his clothes so fast she laughed again, only stopping when his mouth descended, with purpose, on hers.

She'd never get tired of this. Even when she hated him and had thought he'd played her, she still could never resist his kisses. Or his touch. He pulled her gently on top of him and slid his hands up her stockings to her bare thighs.

Her dress pooled around him as his hand slipped under her panties to find her heat. She raised herself slightly to allow him better access. He found her clitoris and circled it until she was desperate for more. As he slid a finger inside her, his phone started ringing and vibrating.

She started and went still. Of all the days...

He grabbed the phone with one hand, and her heart dropped. But he didn't take the call, just placed the edge of the phone against her clit, letting it vibrate against her. She arched as he pulled her panties to one side and slid his dick inside her, his phone still vibrating. "Oh my God," she gasped as he filled her.

The phone stilled and Simon took a fast look at the screen. He grinned and showed her. "Barnum," he said. Her eyes half closed with pleasure. Barnum wouldn't just call once and leave a message; he'd call until it was picked up.

It started vibrating again and he held the whole phone against her as he thrust into her. Need for release rushed through her like a wave. Simon's eyes were on her face.

"You've never looked more beautiful. Wedding dress, me inside you..."

"Barnum making me come...?" she moaned.

"Me making you come," he said, throwing the phone across the room. He withdrew from her and raised her up onto her knees, sliding down so his mouth was level with her panties. He reached for the switchblade he kept in his bedside drawer and cut the satin of the material, exposing her to him. He didn't hesitate. He reached for her and pulled her onto him. His tongue broad-stroked from her ass to her clitoris, making her buck against his mouth.

She braced herself with one arm against the headboard as his assault continued. Then the very tip of his tongue swept across her clit over and over, until she felt like she was bursting inside. As she came, he slid his fingers inside her, prolonging the crest of the wave.

Sadie needed to feel him. Needed to feel his release. She slid down his naked body, grinding for a second on his dick before taking him in hand and sliding him inside her. He held her hips in place as he thrust inside of her over and over. She leaned back and raised her dress. Since Athens, she'd realized that nothing got him off like watching his dick disappear into her.

His thrusts got more urgent. "Sadie," he whispered, as if in awe. Before she could reply, he came in strong spasms.

As they caught their breath, she looked at the scene of the phone crime. "You killed your phone," she said.

"Past time, don't you think?" he said, stroking her thighs. "I'm not going to leave you if you need me, ever again. I realized I'd missed so much of what makes you you. I don't want to do that anymore."

They'd had this conversation before, but it didn't hurt to hear his promise again, mere minutes before their wedding. "Um," she said, looking at her watch and disengaging from him.

"Tell me you're going to marry me with no panties on," he asked, grabbing his clothes and heading for the bathroom.

"I'm going to marry you with no panties," she repeated. She got off the bed, smiling to herself. Brushing down her dress, nicely rumpled now, she looked at herself in the mirror. Not exactly how she'd envisioned getting married, with a sling, a creased dress, and nothing underneath, but it also couldn't have been more perfect.

"Come on. The county lockup awaits our presence." He emerged from the bathroom and held his arm out to her. She tucked her hand in his elbow.

"My mother is going to have a conniption when she finds out we were married at the county jail." She couldn't help but giggle—the county's registrar worked from the jailhouse.

"Isn't that half the fun?" he whispered in her ear.

"Maybe a quarter of the fun," she replied, stopping at the front door.

"What are the other three quarters?" he asked, gazing into her eyes, making her knees wobbly.

"A quarter is that you've taken a sabbatical to stay in Athens for six whole months with me, a quarter is that I'm *finally* marrying you, and a quarter is that I get to milk my injury enough that I get to be on top our *whole* honeymoon."

The truth was that Simon had spoken at length to Barnum and had decided to run one of Delta Force's satellite offices in Europe. Not, unfortunately, in Athens, but close enough that they could easily travel to each other. Less fieldwork for him—the move made him more of a station chief than an operative—which made Sadie a lot happier.

For her part, she'd been promoted—on probation—to Sebastian's desk. She was going back to the office to open all his files and find out what he'd been working on. It was a whole new adventure for her.

"You'll get no complaints from me." He raised an eyebrow pseudosexily.

She poked her tongue out, which he claimed in one swoop.

He took her breath away. All over again.

Turn the page for a preview of *Risk of Exposure*, coming in spring 2016!

He hit enter, and then had a pang of...something. He'd sworn to himself that he wouldn't make fun of his boss's concern about his daughter, but fifteen reports later and it was frankly too hard to keep a lid on his frustration. The sooner his boss realized that she was safe, the sooner Mal could go on to his next job—which would hopefully be more interesting than following the most bloody boring woman in the world around the most bloody boring town in Ukraine.

Abby Baston was one of life's do-gooders. She'd dropped out of college in her first semester to join Aide International and was currently working at a Ukrainian orphanage. She'd been there about six months, and her father was getting increasingly concerned for her safety, after the recent saber-rattling of the Russians.

Mal's instructions were to get her out if the Russians did anything aggressive, like storm the Ukrainian border. Of course the silly woman had chosen an orphanage less than five klicks from the Russian border.

And of course, Mal was spinning his wheels, following her sorry arse around: apartment, run, apartment, orphanage, and apartment again. He wanted to scream at her to get a fucking life. Go somewhere interesting, do something dubious—anything to make this job less boring. She barely smiled or broke stride to even look in a shop window.

And it was fucking hard work, sitting there doing nothing. Under normal circumstances, he'd just engineer a meeting, seduce her, and pretend to be her boyfriend until the job was over. It was a method he'd perfected over time, and by far the easiest way to keep an unsuspecting principal close and safe.

Not to mention the most fun. But she wasn't even interesting enough to warrant even entertaining that idea.

Besides, he valued his job. Baston was one of the few people who didn't bat an eye at Mal's heavily redacted employment record. So this was a job worth keeping, and seducing the boss's daughter was out of the question. Which meant that he actually had to do his job and follow her everywhere she went. And now his life was effectively as boring as hers.

He checked that the sitrep had been received, checked his watch and yawned, leaned back in his plastic lawn chair and propped his feet up on the windowsill of his apartment. A camera was set up on a tripod, for all the good it did. The girl closed the curtains when she came home from the orphanage at night. He sighed and closed his eyes. He'd never been as tired on a job as he was here.

There was just nothing to keep his brain occupied. In the two weeks he'd been in the flat, he'd tried crosswords, Sudoku, and mah-jongg. He hadn't actually tried Candy Crush. He was saving that as a last resort. Even his damn PC was complaining at the shit he was making it do. A quiet buzzer went off beside him and he reluctantly took his feet off the sill and leaned forward, his hand on the remote for the camera.

He'd put the alarm under the carpet in her doorway so that he'd be alerted to anyone entering her flat. Even if it was just her. He checked his watch again. Yup. She was bang on time.

His boss was a wizened old dog who had any number of awful and awesome stories to tell after a drink and a cigar. What the hell had happened to his offspring? His son was some kind of corporate lawyer and his daughter was—well, an aid worker. Where was this generation's love of danger, excitement, and risk?

Okay, it wasn't exactly a different generation; she was only six years younger than him. But still. He leaned back in his rickety chair and contemplated the women he'd had who'd been about six years younger. And then he wondered what Danielle was up to now—she'd been every bit of six years older than him...and those six years were all she'd admitted to. But she'd been a classy—and very dirty—lady. He grinned at the memory. They'd been in the Sinai, he'd been collecting intel, and she did work for the embassy. She'd opened doors to him in the Egyptian society that would have remained closed to someone like him. She was...

What the—

He got up so fast that the lawn chair snapped closed and fell to the floor. Abby was opening the window, despite the chilly evening air. She was jumping up and down. What the—?

The floor-to-ceiling windows showed virtually her whole apartment except the bedroom, which he'd already looked at the first time he'd broken in. He grinned as she waved her hands around. She'd burned something. Ouch, it looked like it had spilled on her. For a second something panged in him, seeing her with something red all down the front of her shirt. A wafer-thin sliver of his brain thought she might've been shot, but the rest of his brain's experience said gunshot victims rarely flapped around like that.

For a second something else flickered across his mind. That tiny sliver of his brain hadn't been surprised at the prospect of her being shot. Mal's eyes flickered to the right for a second as he tried to solidify that thought. There was something about her. Was anyone really that dull in real life? Especially a relative of his boss? Was she hiding something?

He'd survived years of combat and enemy activity just listening to his gut. And his gut was now singing a song that had been alien to him before Abby had spilled something tomato down her front. Accepting that maybe she wasn't exactly as she seemed relaxed him. It was as if his instinct had been waiting for his brain to catch up. He was going to have to meet her.

Somehow.

Eyes on Abby, he opened a bag of strangely flavored Ukrainian crisps...no chance of burning anything in here. He hadn't even touched the kitchen—such as it was—since he'd arrived. He watched the windows of her apartment, newly alert to any possibility.

She disappeared for a few minutes, and he picked up his binoculars.

He looked back up as a movement caught his eye. She'd taken her shirt off and was waving it around her head, trying to get the smoke out of the apartment. In her underwear. He fumbled the binoculars and they fell on his foot. He winced and picked them up, carefully stretching his foot to make sure there was no lasting damage.

Looking across the road, he could still see her waving the smoke away. His fingers twitched toward the binoculars again. Every cell in his body wanted to see her in her underwear, but he knew he shouldn't.

Except...he had a hook in his brain now. Something wasn't right. He just couldn't figure out what.

He peered through the window. Yes he could have gone all zoom lens on her, but knowing she was in her underwear kind of made him feel sketchy about looking. All he needed to do was make sure she was okay, and try to figure out what was starting to bother him about her.

She was laughing at herself. Waving her arms around the room like a crazy person. He smiled. He'd seen her smile only a couple of times, and once had been in an ID photo that was in her file.

Bloody hell!

She started dancing like a crazy person, still wafting smoke out of the window. She wriggled out of her skirt and was also wafting that around her head, making her look from a distance that she was twirling duo lassos. It was like watching a totally different person. In virtually no clothes. He looked away again, but his eyes were inevitably drawn back to the tableau.

She coughed, covering her mouth with her skirt, and he tensed. Was there gas? Was the smoke too much for her? But she just turned back to the kitchen. Then she popped open a few other windows and continued waving her arms to get rid of the residual burning smell probably, laughing and singing, seemingly at the top of her voice. This was totally not the Abby he'd been following for weeks. Not even close. She looked fun.

Determined not to invade her privacy any more, he grabbed his phone and paged through the news. A flash from Abby's window caught his eye, and he looked up again. She was closing the windows and swishing the curtains shut. All but one that didn't go all the way. He watched for a second and then went back to the news—such as it was. Celebrities, politics, and wars. He sighed and clicked through to a story about the G20 meetings that were being held in Athens. He knew a few operatives working there, so he scanned the article for anything familiar.

He took one more cursory look at Abby's apartment.

Oh my God, what is she doing now? This was obviously a

part of her evening routine that he hadn't seen before.

Abby stretched like a cat, yawned, and held some kind of yoga pose. He only saw half her body between the curtains that hadn't completely shut, but still, he couldn't help but notice her breasts move together as she did.

He swallowed. *Look away, look away.*

He looked back.

She turned around and touched her toes. Jesus fucking Christ. Impossibly small panties covered barely anything. His eyes flicked to the binoculars. *No way, Garrett.* He wasn't going to start being a Peeping Tom at his advanced age. God, he wanted to see her though. What did that make him?

And did he really care?

It was like seeing her with a whole new perspective. Okay, she was almost naked, but still—he had to find out more about her, if only to quell his gut. He started to second-guess himself. Was he reaching for an excuse to actually meet her? Was he fooling himself into believing he had a gut feeling that something wasn't as it seemed?

He looked again, resolutely leaving the binoculars on the floor.

He was a fucking saint.

Her dark, wavy hair was pinned up in some kind of bun, and the reading glasses she wore seriously made Mal think he was watching *True Confessions of a Librarian Behind Closed Doors.* There must be a reality show like that somewhere in the world.

Between the swaying curtains that half-hid her, she slid gently and slowly into the splits. She bent and touched her arms to her left foot, and then to her right, and then to her left again.

She brought her legs together in front of her, and then stood. She turned so her back was toward the window, and swung her arms around, holding each shoulder with her other hand, as if they were sore. Rolling her neck from side to side, she took out the...whatever was holding her hair up, and let the curls fall down her back.

His mouth went dry. She was beautiful. Not her hair, or face, or body, although now he was getting a good look, he couldn't deny their allure, but it was her grace that really took hold of him. It was as if there were two Abbys. The one who never cracked a smile, who followed a precise routine and never seemed as if she was capable of fun. The other could laugh at herself, even when the kitchen was on fire. She danced and sang and laughed. And then the way she held her arms, the legs that were obviously as strong as they were long. How her back looked when she stretched, long muscles moving under her skin.

He wondered what her skin felt like.

And wondered why he'd briefly thought it normal that she might have been shot.

She turned back to the window and reached behind her back as if she was about to take off her bra. He stood, stock still, almost holding his breath. But her head jerked to the side, and she stopped what she was doing and walked over to a side table. She picked up the phone.

Damn that caller to hell. Damn him.

He took a breath, realizing he was as hard as he'd ever

been, not actually physically touching someone.

He wanted to meet her. To explore his gut feeling about her. Sure. That was why.

Abby closed the curtains all the way, suddenly realizing that if anyone in the opposite building was home—which, judging by the lack of lights, didn't seem likely—they'd be able to see straight into her apartment, and probably judge her for her lack of cooking skills. To be honest, it could only loosely be called "cooking."

How do you burn tomato soup? Then, how would it be possible to try to move it so fast from the stove that it slopped over on to your only white blouse? She had no idea what was up with her today, but cooking was not on the cards. The smoke had already blackened the ceiling over the stove, and she wondered for a second what would happen if the CIA couldn't get their deposit back. She snorted softly to herself. Drone strike? A visit from "the guys"?

The smoke had left the apartment, leaving a sweet, charred smell that she hoped would also leave soon. Good thing she wasn't field-stripping guns, or having to pass aptitude tests. She'd been so clumsy recently. She was out of practice. With everything.

She'd had this insane idea that someone was watching her, but she'd never seen anyone, and no one had intercepted her when she'd left to dead-drop information under the guise of going for a run. She'd looked for a good week before deciding that she was imagining it. The problem with being a covert officer—a solitary profession at the best of times—is that it made you slightly paranoid. Sometimes correctly, but most often not.

She stretched again and grinned to herself. She never imagined she'd be given a job so dull that an imaginary tail would be a welcome distraction. But regardless, the border—and whoever crossed it—was her only focus.

The orphanage—her cover—held a surveillance point, what she called her "little watch tower," so she could keep her eye on the border.

She was just north of the "Russian-backed fighters" and the Ukrainians who were having sporadic firefights in the towns and countryside. Thing was, no one knew if the fighters were really "Russian-backed" or they were part of Russia's legitimate army. If it was the latter and Abby could get proof, then the might of NATO's combined armies would converge to get Ukraine's army back. It was probably the most important job she'd ever been given and she was going to effing ace it. Even if her hosts were less than impressed that she was there.

She switched off the water and stood staring at the shower wall for a second. For these six months she'd only had contact with her landlord, Tanoff, and his disapproving wife, Brigda. Well, and the kids in the orphanage, but that didn't really count since her hybrid Ukrainian/Russian that they spoke in the area was somewhat rusty.

Six long months on her own. She wanted to talk to someone. Just to see if she could smile still. If those muscles still worked. She wanted to touch someone. Even if it was an accidental brush of fingers. As she dried her hair, she practiced smiling in the mirror. It was pitiful. Fake; and not to put too fine a point on it, it looked as if it pained her to smile.

Once she'd worked from the U.S. embassy in Moscow. She'd arrived in winter and the first thing she'd noticed is that no one smiled. Not in the street, not in the stores, not even in the embassy. It was as if an air of suppression rested on everyone in the country. An artic freeze, she supposed. Only vodka brought smiles. And that was only if it was the good stuff. And those smiles only lasted until the bottle became empty. It was the same here. She blamed the proximity to the Russian border.

Maybe she'd go out tomorrow night. To that bar a few streets away that she passed on her way to the orphanage. She'd double-check the street name on her way to work tomorrow. Even if she only spoke to the bartender, it would be one more person on her scant list of contacts that she was supposed to fill out daily. She hated to think just how boring the analysts at Langley would think her. Or maybe she'd go to the restaurant she'd been to a couple of times when she'd had no food in the house. Whatever she did, she needed to socialize with someone. Anyone. And soon.

About the Author

Emmy Curtis is an editor and a romance writer. An expat Brit, she quells her homesickness with Cadbury Flakes and Fray Bentos pies. She's lived in London, Paris, and New York and has settled for the time being in North Carolina. When not writing, Emmy loves to travel with her military husband and take long walks with their Lab. All things considered, her life is chock-full of hoot and just a little bit of nanny. And if you get that reference...well, she already considers you kin.

Learn more at:

EmmyCurtis.com

Facebook.com/EmmyCurtisAuthor

Twitter: @EmmyCurtis19

CPSIA information can be obtained
at www.ICGtesting.com
Printed in the USA
LVOW12s2237280816
502232LV00001B/10/P

9 781455 564125